CHAPTER ONE

Wyoming Territory
June 1869

The buckskin raised it's head, snorting it's discontent at its forced leisure, wanting instead to follow its inbred instincts and be on the move, its ears pricked for action as it eyed the herd with restlessness. The toasty warm-colored tan horse was a temperamental beast for certain and could most definitely be considered high-spirited, but regardless he still lacked nothing in control or performance. It could outwork and outlast any other horse on the ranch and almost seemed intent on proving that point every chance it got.

Cord Chantry sat atop the magnificent animal as he took in the Hereford cattle he had been entrusted by his employer with bringing to market. He had missed his previous horse, a paint of unmatched speed and endurance that he had lost to an ill-fated encounter with a pit of rattlesnakes. But though he longed to be on the back of his beloved paint, he had bonded with the buckskin much easier than he had anticipated. He had acquired the buckskin only a few, short months prior, but its performance on the range had not been disappointing, not in the least. He had been reluctant to put so much stock in another animal after having admired his previous horse so much, but this one was different. The buckskin knew what was required of him and was determined not to give anything less even without the need to be pushed.

He was a man of simple demands. His hard and troubled upbringing spanning from his drunken, abusive father to his absent whore of a mother having molded him into the subdued man he was today, albeit forcing him into manhood at a much younger age than it should have. Being the only child he had been forced to grow up early and learn at a very young age to fend for himself for there were no others around him that he could rely on. He had grown up fast, too fast to learn the ways and wants of the world and innocent in the challenges and dangers that a young man faces when they are forced to grow up too quickly in a man's world. He had grown up hard and tough with nothing being given to him and everything gotten through hard work and blinding stubbornness. He was resilient which was perhaps the only thing that had kept him alive through the years.

Cord had tried his hand at scouting the Wyoming Territory for awhile and had experienced marginal success in it, enjoying his contribution to helping those looking to set up their new lives in the territory, but he had never felt as happy and alive as when he were on the back of a horse punching cattle. It had been this way for half of his twenty-seven years and long ago he had come to realize that it would likely be that way until he could no longer climb into a saddle. When that day came, he figured he might as well be adorned in his Sunday best and placed in the ground for he would be of no use to anyone in any other capacity.

At six-foot two, Cord Chantry was an imposing figure on

a mount with his crystal grey eyes squinting from the unforgiving sun and his black hair tousled from under his black Stetson. His back was broad and hardened from years of punching cattle and mending fences, his large hands calloused and toughened like the leather saddle that adorned his buckskin.

Growing up he had learned to trust no one, especially women, for all of the women in his life had disappointed and hurt him in one way or another so that he was not willing to let another get close enough to him to chance having it happen to him all over again. Because off this, his defensive demeanor was often interpreted as being someone who was standoffish and unapproachable. He did not wish to be distant, but having to relay his intentions were not easy for him and, therefore, the misconceptions were never addressed, leaving him with very few friends. But those that knew him knew that he was a honorable man of good character and honesty who was loyal to his friends to the end. He was a man whose word was as good as gold and would just as soon be shot than to be accused of being guilty of a lie. His strong, chiseled features turned the heads of any women he encountered, but none of that mattered because these days his eyes were only interested in turning the head of one woman, Madeline Stafford.

Three years his junior, Madeline Stafford was twice the woman of any he had ever crossed paths with in his entire life. Her strength and confidence appealed to him as much, if not more, than her beauty. Her dark brown hair and matching eyes drew their own attention from other men, men who envied Cord for being the one lucky enough to be with her. She was a deliberate woman who never made a move without having a purpose behind it, a quality that Cord Chantry admired greatly. He had fallen for her and fallen hard, a feat that he had long ago abandoned as ever being a possibility

given his distrust in women rooted by the betrayal and abandonment of his own mother. He knew enough to know that
meeting someone so appealing was a once in a lifetime experience which is why as soon as he was able he planned to
make her his own.

"Cord! Cord Chantry!" a voice called out from off to the
side of him, the mention of his name bringing him around.

"Yeah!" Cord responded as he shook off his thoughts and
pulled the buckskin's reins in the direction of the voice.

"Are you with us today, buddy?" the man jokingly asked
as he pulled up beside Cord, his horse anxiously hopping
about in small circles as it impatiently waited for it's rider to
initiate its next move. "I've been calling your name, but
you're just sittin' there staring off at the herd all glassy-
eyed."

"Sorry," Cord apologized with a somewhat sheepish grin.
"I guess I was somewhere else."

"You were thinking about *her* again, weren't ya?" The man
teased as he continued to fight to contain his horse's bridled
enthusiasm.

"Yeah, I guess I was."

Tell Witherspoon grinned from the embarrassment he
had successfully inflicted upon his friend. "Man, you've got it
bad."

"I'm gonna ask her to marry me," Cord announced
proudly from out of nowhere as he looked at Tell for his
reaction.

"Hey, that's great, Cord!" Tell said enthusiastically with a
smile. "Congratulations!"

"Don't congratulate me too soon," Cord warned. "She
hasn't said 'yes', yet."

"She will, don't worry," his friend assured him. "Why
wouldn't she say 'yes'?" Tell added. "You two are perfect for
each other."

"Well, let's just hope that she's as optimistic about that as you are."

Tell Witherspoon flashed a encouraging grin and spun his horse around promptly heading towards the herd with Cord following right behind him, his mind once again deep in thought. The decision to propose to Madeline had been a long time coming for Cord and was something he was passionate about, the first thing he had been passionate about for quite some time, longer than he could remember. He felt as if she felt the same way about him as he did her, but as strong and confident as he was about his decision-making skills there was always that nagging question in the recesses of his mind that taunted him and made him question whether she really did. Was there a woman who could love him, truly love him unconditionally? One that he could actually depend on that would not let him down or leave him? Till now, he had believed them not to exist. He felt as if Madeline Stafford would be the one exception.

All he knew was he wanted to spend the rest of his life with this woman which was something he had never felt about anyone else and knew he would never feel again. He had thought that his own parent's tumultuous relationship would have soured his opinion on marriage and kept the thought from ever entering his mind, but Madeline Stafford coming into his life had somehow managed to overcome those doubts. He had a chance here at real happiness and he was going to take it before he woke up and found out that it was only a dream.

Cord Chantry's mind shook himself back to the work at hand as he went back to focusing on the herd, his outlook brightened just from informing Tell of his plans, the only person who knew of them. It had been less than a year since Cord had met Tell during his trip on the stage from Jackson Creek to Benton Springs, but in that short amount of time he had grown to like the young man as if he had known him for much longer. They had met when Cord was running from Frank Quincey and his gang...*Frank Quincey. The very thought of the man's name still incited rage within him*...after Cord had killed Quincey's baby brother in a failed stagecoach robbery. As a result, Quincey had been ruthless in his pursuit of them, chasing him all the way to Hurley where things almost came to an end for Cord and his friends. A wounded Frank Quincey had been carried off by his accomplices, to where he was not sure and no one had seen or heard from him since, which was fine with Cord. The only saving grace in that period of his life was that it was also the time when he had met Madeline Stafford.

She had been reserved at first, and even thought him to be of a peculiar nature and had admitted to such once they had grown to know each other better. But after the incident with Quincey she and Cord had settled into the same town of Benton Springs and their relationship had taken a turn from that of nothing more than being mere acquaintances in an unfortunate incident to something much more. Fate had intervened and Cord's life had been changed forever.

Cord Chantry continued to work the herd corralling a few strays that had wandered off the path and bringing them back around, his horse instinctively nudging the ornery beasts on towards a final destination of the stockyards in Hurley. It had been some time since he had visited there and although the town had a bad history with him he was still looking forward to once again seeing his old friends Sheriff Sage Connelly and Deputy Tom Wills.

The cattle took advantage of the range opening up and like melting butter they caressed the hillsides moving with ease from the experienced hands driving them onward. The herd was small by all standards, only some three-hundred plus head of quality Hereford stock, but despite the

minimal size it was still important to get them to the stockyards on time so they could board the afternoon train for
Fort Griffin and its men. With winter coming in the not-
too-distant future the soldiers and civilians there would
need meat to sustain them through the hard times and the
Walking A's contract with the Cavalry provided for just
that.

The afternoon sky was clear with only small patches of
clouds dotting the overhead like balls of cotton. Summer was
fully upon them, though the worst of it was still more than a
month or so away. It was hard to imagine that a territory so
lit up with summer blossoms and shortgrass prairies of blue
grama and Buffalo grass could transform into such a brutal
and unforgiving landscape where snow froze so densely that
the stagecoaches would be able to ride on top of it, if they
had been able to move about at all.

Cord Chantry was grateful for the cooperation of the
weather which had not been helpful till now, but whose
changes had made the drive that much easier to endure and
helped them to stay on schedule. The cattle drivers also
appreciated the interruption of rainfall as the hooves of so
many animals were doing considerable damage to the grazing.
That would minimize available grass and become problematic
for their herds in the winter and for any free range herds that
happened to follow them soon thereafter.

As the outskirts of Hurley came into their view, the men
felt a glimmer of relief wash over them. Soon, their job here
would be satisfied and they would use the down time to take
in the action of a different town for a change. At the same
time, Cord was anxious to get back to Madeline. He thought
about how his priorities had changed so just because of her.
In the past, he would have dismissed any interest he had in
her and moved on, fearing that she would let him down or
hurt him. But Madeline was different. Their friendship had

evolved into love and he now knew that he wanted to spend the rest of his life with her.

The herd poured into the busy streets of Hurley interrupting its atmosphere and bringing the movement of the townspeople to an abrupt halt. They had grown accustomed to these types of interruptions, a small price to pay for a town's advancements and growth, knowing that the presence of each herd only worked to solidify the prosperity of Hurley. With the size of the herd being minimal the delay would be short and then life in the bustling town would resume without giving the interruption a second thought.

The cattle drivers made quick time of their arrival and within a short period of time had carefully maneuvered the manageable herd through the streets and into the stockyards. While the foreman handled the paper trail created by the transfer of cattle, the men retired to the streets, joyously tying off their horses and getting an early start on their downtime. Instead of joining them, Cord Chantry decided to take the opportunity to stop by and see the sheriff and his deputy.

CHAPTER TWO

Cord Chantry walked the buckskin the short distance to the sheriff's office, not wanting to place anymore wear on his bad leg than was absolutely necessary. He had learned to favor it, even when he had spent considerable time in the saddle, the result of being shot twice in it within the same day by two different individuals, Frank Quincey and one of his men. Although riding should not have placed stress on the healed wounds the incessant bouncing in the saddle was still enough to evoke a dull discomfort that would stay with him for hours to come. It was something he could unfortunately look forward to each and every time he rode for the rest of his time.

As he threw his leg over the buckskin and eased his tender left leg onto the ground the sheriff and his deputy came walking out of the sheriff's office, both sporting a smile at the sight of their friend.

"How's it going, Cord?" Sheriff Sage Connelly asked as he extended his hand.

"Good to see you, Sage," Cord stated as he proudly shook

hands with the man before turning to the deputy. "Tom, good to see you."

"Good to see you, too, Cord," Deputy Tom Wills responded with a handshake.

Cord looked back at Sage Connelly. "How've you been? How's the side?"

Connelly gently placed his hand on the spot where he had also been shot during the skirmish with Frank Quincey and his men. "Still a little tender to the touch. Doc says it'll always give me trouble. So how are you doing? How's the leg?"

"Not bad," Cord responded. "I can tell when it's going to rain and the cold affects it some, but otherwise I'm good."

"What brings you to Hurley?" Sheriff Connelly asked with a glint of curiosity.

"Just bringing in a small herd. It's the third one, back to back, that we've moved. The first two were from one range to another. While we're in town the foreman decided the fellas needed a little down time before we hit it hard again."

The three men spent the next few minutes conversing on a variety of subjects and updating one another on the recent events in their lives. It felt good for Cord to catch with his friends, an opportunity that he, Cord, admitted he hadn't done often enough. Finally, the discussion was brought back around to his surprised visit.

"Well, I'm glad you stopped by," Sheriff Connelly admitted. "It's been kind of quiet around here lately."

"Don't you prefer that?" Cord asked jokingly.

"Well, yeah, I certainly prefer it to what happened here the last time we had an incident in town."

"No kidding."

Cord's thoughts went back to the day of the shootout with Frank Quincey and his men, a day that he had relived countless times, both while awake and in his dreams. *How could he forget?* Quincey had followed him to Hurley to exact revenge for Cord killing his baby brother. Things had gone badly and many men had died. It was a day that he would never forget, a day filled with mixed emotions. It was the day Cord had met Sheriff Connelly and Deputy Wills, some of the very few that he could call his friends. It was also the day he missed out on killing Frank Quincey, a disappointment that still haunted him.

"So where you headed after this?" Deputy Tom Wills asked curiously.

"I thought I'd hang around town for awhile. Maybe get a drink. I asked my boss if I could take some time off."

Sheriff Sage Connelly and Deputy Wills simultaneously exchanged silent glances before Sheriff Connelly looked back over to Cord. "You're hanging around town?"

Cord picked up on the odd exchange between the two men, but decided to forgo asking about it and leave the gesture out of the conversation. "Yeah. Nathan Brooks lives around here. I heard he finally settled down here and took a job as a blacksmith. Doing really well from what I under-stand. You remember Nathan, don't ya'?"

"Yeah," Sheriff Connelly nodded his head and responded hesitantly as if he were unsure what to do with the informa-tion. "Colored guy. Really stocky build."

"Yeah, that's him," Cord said assuredly.

"I haven't seen him since the shootout with Frank Quincey," Deputy Wills answered.

"Yeah, hard to believe that was almost a year ago," Cord reminisced, his memories mixed with pain and regret. "I wanted to go see how Nathan's doing, maybe have a drink with him, y'know, catch up on old times."

"That sounds good," the sheriff said before he looked off to the side, as if he were uncomfortable in what he was about to say. "Say, Cord, you got a minute to come inside?" Sheriff Sage Connelly asked out of nowhere.

Cord glanced over at Deputy Tom Wills whose expression had fallen, leaving Cord to wonder why their talking had suddenly taken a serious tone. He noticed that Sheriff Connelly's disposition had also grown strangely quiet.

"Yeah, sure," Cord agreed, full of curiosity, as he followed the two men into the sheriff's office. He was surprised to hear Sheriff Connelly closing the door behind him as he picked out a chair for Cord to sit in. Sage walked around and took the seat behind his desk as Deputy Wills took a spot on the corner of it to sit. The whole encounter was starting to concern Cord as he saw a burdened interest in their eyes. "What's going on, Sage?"

Sheriff Sage Connelly shot a quick glance over to Deputy Wills before he answered. "I thought you should know I got word that River Holloway is in town."

The news hit Cord hard. *River Holloway. The man responsible for needlessly killing young Billy Richmond in cold blood.* The very thought of the man's name caused Cord's blood to boil. He fought back the explosion of anger that he wanted to release out of sheer frustration. Finally, Cord was able to calm himself down enough to form a question. "When...when did he get here?"

"He came through here on the stage about a week-and-a-half to two weeks ago," Sheriff Connelly answered. "Stage stopped over for a while. Your fella talked himself into joining a card game in one of the saloons. Before long, there was an argument that this gambler was cheating."

"Was he?" Cord inquired.

"Don't know for sure, but the fellas he was playing with were sure convinced that he was. I know some of 'em, know 'em well enough to know that they don't go around accusing someone of something as serious as that without having proof. Bartender had to call Tom in there to break it up before things got ugly. Tom said the fella was tall, fancy duds and had a strong Creole accent and that his name was 'River'. It's gotta be your boy. Don't know of anyone else with that kind of name."

"Yeah," Cord admitted in a disappointed tone, "that sure sounds like him, alright."

"Well, Tom ran him out of there. He left on the next stage heading to Maysville, but he snuck back into town a few days later. I wired the sheriff there in Maysville to warn him, but he wired back and said that the gambler had already left town and then we spotted him back here again in a different saloon. Haven't heard any more complaints about him so we don't know if he's still around or not."

Cord eyed the sheriff as he had listened intently. Sage Connelly was a cautious man, a practical and dependable man who had holstered the tension in the town of Hurley and kept the peace with very little more than a reputation backing him up that had clearly been proven to be true. Sage had come to Hurley years before and saw the recklessness and abandonment of law and order and decided he wanted to do something about it. When the current sheriff was murdered with no one ever being charged, Sage had had enough and stepped into the position. He cleaned up the streets of Hurley and had managed to maintain the peace here ever since. Anyone coming to Hurley to cause trouble knew that as long as Sage Connelly was sheriff it wasn't a good move for their future, which made sense why he had River run out of town the first time. Still, Cord just couldn't understand why his friend was sharing this news.

"I know you're wondering why I'm telling you all of this, Cord. I'm telling you because I don't want to see you get yourself in the middle of something that you can't get out of. If you hang around town there's a good chance that you'll end up in the saloon and if you do there's a good chance that you'll run into this fella. Even if you stay away you're still likely to come across him sooner or later, especially if your friend is running the blacksmith shop." Sheriff Connelly leaned his forearms onto his desk with his hands interlocked in front of him. "I'm telling you this, Cord, so you won't run into him and do something that you'll regret."

"He killed Billy Richmond," Cord stated flatly.

"But that happened out in the territory, not in the city limits of Hurley."

"It doesn't matter where it was. It happened right in front of me, Sage. I saw it. Maddie saw it. Everyone there saw it."

"I understand you're upset, Cord, but I don't have jurisdiction out there," Sheriff Connelly argued.

Cord took in a deep breath to try to quell his growing agitation. "I know you don't have jurisdiction out there, Sage, but *somebody* does. Get the federal marshall out here and let *him* handle it. That's what he gets paid for, isn't it?"

"It's not that easy, Cord. The federal marshall is spread pretty thin. He has an entire territory to cover..."

Cord stood and interrupted Sheriff Connelly's point as he paced back towards the wall behind him, his temper pushing him to the limit of concealing it.

Sheriff Connelly continued. "...to cover and he doesn't always have time to come out to investigate every single shooting."

Cord turned and stared at his friend. "Every shooting or just this one?"

Sheriff Connelly stiffened in his chair, his voice becoming rigid. "Now, that's not fair, Cord. You're not thinking rationally right now, I get it. But don't go implying that I'm not doing my job."

"I'm not doing that, Sage, you know that, but it's just frustrating to know that he killed a man, actually someone not much older than a boy, and he's going to walk away with no repercussions."

"I'm sorry, Cord, I wish I was in a position to do something, but my hands are tied."

Cord started for the door. "Well, mine aren't."

Sheriff Connelly stood abruptly. "Cord, I know what you're thinking and you'd better just get that thought out of your head right now."

"Sage, he killed a man!"

"I know, Cord, and if the federal marshall were here we could swear out a complaint against him."

"A *complaint?*" Cord argued. "Are you kidding? He doesn't deserve a complaint! He doesn't deserve any kind of consideration!"

Sheriff Connelly walked around his desk and over to Cord as he spoke. "Listen to me, Cord. Don't go after this man. I'm not asking you this as a sheriff, I'm asking you this as a friend. I'm trying to warn you. I can only protect you so much and after that my hands are tied. If you..."

Cord started for the door and Sheriff Connelly grabbed his arm to stop him. "...*if* you go after this man, I'm telling you right now that I can't help you. You'll be putting yourself on the wrong side of the law and if you choose to do that then I won't have any choice but to do my job and bring you in to stand trial. You can't take the law into your own hands no matter how badly you may want to." Cord started to pull away from his hold, but Sheriff Connelly tightened his grip even more. "Do you hear what I'm saying, Cord? You'll be on your own."

Cord looked deep into the man's eyes. "I've been on my own my whole life, Sage. This won't be any different." He could tell the sheriff was torn. He tried to ease the burden of what he knew his friend would be forced to do. "You do what you have to do, Sage. I won't take it personally. I promise."

Sheriff Connelly refused to release Cord's arm from his grip. "Cord, listen to me. I know this fella deserves to pay for what he did to your friend. I get that. But you can't make this your personal vendetta. It isn't worth it, regardless of you thinking that it is. Don't do something that you'll wish you hadn't even though you think it's the right thing to do. Don't let your emotions about this cloud your judgment. Please. Let this go."

Cord looked at his friend and then over at Deputy Wills. He could see the worry in their faces, worry that he would do something he would deeply regret and that he would not be able to walk away from. He succumbed to reason and decided it wasn't worth it.

"Alright, Sage. We'll do it your way. I'll leave River alone. But you have to promise me that you'll contact the federal marshall and bring him here. River can't just get away with this."

"You have my word," Sage agreed with a relieved smile. "Now, enough of this sad talk. What do you say? Can Tom and I buy you a drink?"

"Thanks, but I need to get going. I need to get back to the ranch. Maybe some other time"

"Sure. If you can, drop by later."

"Thanks." Cord nodded to Sage and gave a smiling glance over to Deputy Wills as he walked out the door. He felt an overwhelming need to find River Holloway and kill him, but he promised he wouldn't.

CHAPTER THREE

*'...everyone step away from your horses and your rifles,' River stated
firmly.
Billy went for his gun and River fired, striking Billy in the upper
chest and knocking him back onto the ground,
his shirt immediately beginning to stain from the blood as he grimaced
from the intense pain.
Madeline saw the horror and screamed.
Cord tried to move to check on Billy, but River cocked the revolver
again, stopping him in his tracks.
'I have to check on him!' Cord pleaded.
'He'll be fine, I assure you,' River stated coldly in his thick Creole
accent...*

*'How is he?' Madeline asked him as Cord knelt by Billy's side.
'He's lost a lot of blood. I think he's going into shock. He can't keep
going on like this.'
'How is young William?' Holbrook Sanders asked.*

'He's not doing well," Madeline relayed the answer as she glanced down at him.

'What are we going to do?' Madeline asked.

'I don't know. He won't make it if we keep forcing him to ride.'

'I'll stay behind.'

'You won't have to. Billy's dead.'

'Billy's dead...'

'Billy's dead...'

Cord was startled awake, struggling to breathe, taking in great gasps of air to try to satisfy what his lungs were so desperately craving. His body was drenched in sweat, his entire frame heated up, but his skin remained surprisingly cool to the touch. It was the nightmare again. It had been happening off and on since Billy Richmond had died, been killed. Cord had tried to ignore it, but it was happening more and more as time passed. He wanted to believe that someday it would go away, but it certainly didn't seem to be doing so.

It took him several seconds to calm down his heart trying to beat its way out of his chest before he realized that it was nothing more than a dream. A nightmare, one that he had been forced to relive again and again. But it was so real. *How could that have not been real?*

Finally, he tossed back the sweat-drenched cover and swung his legs off of the bed and onto the floor as he sat up, his body still lurching from the trauma of the dream's realism. He cupped his face into his hands as he tried to balance out his erratic breathing, slowly calming himself back towards normal. Running his hands through his wet hair he became irritated by its dampness and wiped them on his shirt only to succeed in transferring more wetness onto his hands.

Afraid that his commotion had awakened someone Cord

glanced around at the other sleeping cowhands, none of which had stirred. *Good. He would hate to have to admit that he had experienced a nightmare since he didn't feel like offering an explanation and felt even less inclined to hear ribbing about it, even if it were out of good-natured fun.*

He sat on the side of his bed for several minutes until he had gathered his senses. He understood that Sage was his friend and that he was only trying to protect him and he knew that the man would only act if forced to do so by something Cord did. But none of that mattered. To hell with what was right and what was legal. This wasn't the time for that. This was more about what was deserved. He had given his word to Sage, but despite that, he couldn't take this anymore. It shouldn't have been this hard to get over this but it had been. He was tired of seeing innocent people being harmed or even killed by others and get away with it just because they could. He had witnessed the senseless killing of others almost his entire life and he had grown sick of it. His dream was just the resolve that he needed. It was his mind telling him to follow his heart. Now he had no choice. He was sure that he knew what he had to do.

He had to bring River Holloway in.

The sun topped over the mountains, raining light down into the far-reaching valley below, the instant heat it created starting to burning off the crispness of the ground which was still covered in dew-covered grass. In the corner of the front yard a rooster performed his duties as he called the ranch awake while an errant steer in a nearby pasture answered in his own bellowing response.

The door of the bunkhouse slowly opened as ranch hands began groggily filing out, some adjusting their suspenders onto their shoulders while others lazily scratched their heads before adorning their hats over their unforgiving bed hair. The crispness of the morning slowly went to work to awaken the bunch as they all made their way over to their assigned duties of the Walking A ranch.

Cattle had become the lifeblood of the territory and continued to be the largest commodity. Cattlemen in the area had come to realize that the cattle of the Wyoming territory had evolved into animals that could survive the treacherous winters without the need for supplemental feed. These herds could rely on the nutrient-rich native grasses to sustain them through the harsh winter months and with ample water available to them, it was the ideal situation for both cattle and cattle ranches. With the introduction of the Union Pacific railroad through Cheyenne, moving cattle was made much easier and quicker and became responsible for cattle ranches sprouting up everywhere within the territory. One such ranch was the Walking A.

The expansive Walking A ranch was owned by Joden Gallagher, a rancher who had migrated from Northern Texas years earlier. In the midst of the Civil War, Union Armies controlled the Mississippi River which subsequently caused shipments of beef to the east to halt. That calamity paired with having so many young men leaving their ranches to fight in the war caused the cattle industry there to suffer greatly. Gallagher decided he needed to make a fresh start for himself, one that would ensure a successful future for he and his family. Taking his herd of Texas Longhorns, Gallagher and his men moved them north to Albany County in the Wyoming Territory and never looked back. Within a few short years, his foresight was responsible for his ranch being transformed into one of the largest and most profitable ones in the entire territory.

Cord Chantry had worked for Joden Gallagher years earlier when Gallagher was just starting out helping Gallagher build his vision and watched the Walking A transform from one man's dream to reality. But despite his content in being there Cord's immaturity got the better of him and he became anxious to see what lay beyond the fences he had worked so hard to help put up so he left to chase the unknown for a better way of life. When he realized that his heart was back at the Walking A, he contacted Gallagher and asked for his old job back. Gallagher was more than happy to oblige. That was almost a year ago and Cord Chantry had never been happier.

Inside the expansive ranch house, Joden Gallagher made his way down the wide, oak staircase to the living room below. The room was broad and filled with numerous mementos that he had amassed throughout his years of building his ranch, each one being rooted from a story that he was still able to recall a majority of the time, although sometimes not quite as well as he had just a few years earlier.

Next to the living room was the library, which also doubled as his office and provided a large fieldstone fireplace where he spent many a night sitting in his broad-backed leather chair staring into the flames and reading from his extensive collection of books, one of his most prized possessions, while casually sipping brandy or enjoying a robust cigar. He had fallen asleep in that chair more times than he could remember, it's soothing effects nursed by the serenity of the fire was more than enough to take away the edge of the perils created by owning and managing such a large operation as was his.

His path past the library and into the kitchen took longer these days than it had before when he had first built his home as middle age took its toll on his frame. Decades of strenuous ranch work had managed to whittle down his once imposing figure into a more diminished, more fragile individual. At sixty-one, he could very easily be considered an old man by normal standards except for the fact that the same arduous work that had inflicted so much damage to his body over the years had also toughened him and made him somewhat resistant to the relentless effects of aging, at least for the time being. He might have been unable to keep up with his younger counterparts, but regardless he could still hold his own quite impressively for a man his age.

Joden Gallagher sat down at the head of the massive carved oak table as his wife, Clarice, entered from the kitchen carrying a plate of freshly cooked eggs, biscuits and bacon in one hand and a stemming cup of black coffee in her other as she had done for their entire forty-one years of marriage. Although the other meals in the ranch house were prepared by their cook, Clarice still preferred to continue with such an arrangement and had grown accustomed to spending this quality time with her husband before the start of another long day and planned to do so until the day they were separated by destiny.

"Good morning, my love," she spoke as he leaned over and they shared a kiss before she placed the food in front of him and then sat down in the nearest chair.

"Good morning," he returned with a smile. "Thank you," he added as he took a cautious sip of his coffee before picking up his fork to begin eating.

"So what do you have planned today?" she inquired as she watched her husband enjoy the fruits of her labor.

Joden Gallagher waited to swallow his mouthful before he could answer. "We need to move some cattle over from the valley over to the south pasture. All that rain we just got softened up the grass in there something terrible. If we don't get 'em relocated that grass won't be useable for the rest of the year." He was about to go into more detail when they heard a knock at the front door. Joden started to get up, but Clarice placed her hand in front of him. "You stay put and eat your breakfast, old man. I'll get it." She walked over and opened the door to find Cord Chantry standing there, his hat respectfully in his hands.

"Ah, good morning, Cord," she said with a broad smile.

"Morning, Mrs. Gallagher," Cord responded as he nervously rotated the rim of his hat in his hand. "Is Mr. Gallagher busy?"

"Why, no, he's just started breakfast. Come on in."

Cord started to take a step inside, but got second thoughts. "I don't want to interrupt his meal. I can just come back later."

"Who is it, Clarice?" came Joden Gallagher's voice from the dining room.

Clarice Gallagher turned her head in his direction. "It's Cord, dear. He says he needs to see you."

"Tell him to come on in," Joden Gallagher insisted.

"Come in, Cord," she insisted as she stepped off to the side to allow him access to the house. "You know where the dining room is," she added with a smile.

"Thank you, ma'am," Cord said as he sheepishly entered the home and began walking through the living room to where Joden Gallagher was eating. When he reached the far end of the table, he stopped.

"Morning, Cord," Joden said with a grin. "How 'bout some breakfast?"

"No, thank you, Mr Gallagher," Cord answered timidly. "I just came to ask a favor of 'ya."

Joden Gallagher sat down his fork to give Cord his full attention and picked up his cup of coffee. "What is it?" he asked before taking a hesitant sip.

"I was wondering if I could have the day off," Cord started. "I have some business over in Hurley that I need to take care of."

"How long will you be gone?"

"Hopefully, just for the day."

"It's none of my business, but is everything alright?"

"Yessir. I just need to go handle something personal."

"Well, I'm not one to stand in the way of a man's private business so I guess I'll see you tomorrow."

CHAPTER FOUR

Cord Chantry rode his buckskin back into the bustling town of Hurley, a smaller town than some of the others in the Wyoming territory, but still not lacking in potential growth. His attention was already on alert for any signs of River Holloway even though he knew River would never be out in the open, being more of an inside man as such. Cord doubted that River had ever been forced to do a hard day's work in his life and would likely fail miserably if he had to. His kind always did. Instead, they chose the easiest lifestyle they could find with the belief that the less exertion they had to endure, the better regardless if whether or not it came at the expense of others.

The ride from Benton Springs to Hurley seemed to take much longer than Cord remembered even though he wasn't herding cattle there, probably due to the building anticipation within him to find River. He had managed to fight back his original plan which was to kill River on sight, an ending he felt River so richly deserved, but he had finally managed to convince himself that doing so would not be the right resolution and would only succeed in bringing trouble down on himself. Instead, his new plan was to locate River and bring him back to the jail in Benton Springs until the federal marshall could be summoned there and River could stand trial. It was not the ideal situation to have to keep watch over River until the marshall could arrive, but it was all he had at the moment. If need be, he would ask Sheriff Connelly to hold River over in Hurley and utilize Sheriff Connelly's jail until the marshall could arrive.

Cord's appearance as a lone stranger to town drew the attention of those who were out and about on the streets as they stopped and took in this new arrival. The buckskin sauntered his way down the lazy street until he was in front of the first of the town's three saloons. Cord took one final glance around and climbed down from his saddle, slightly favoring his bad leg as it touched down onto the dusty street. He panned his vision one last time before stepping up onto the boardwalk and walking through the swinging doors of the Gold Nugget Saloon.

It took a few seconds for his eyes to adjust from the brightness of the afternoon sun to the restrained, darkened atmosphere of the saloon but as soon as he could he walked over to the bar and motioned to the bartender before turning and scanning the contents of the room while he waited for the man's attention. The sound of a bottle being set down onto the wooden bar behind him brought Cord's attention back around to the bartender who had already poured him a shot of whiskey.

"I'm looking for someone," Cord informed the bartender as the man topped off his shot glass.

"Who might that be?" the bartender responded as he sat down the bottle and looked at him with a disinterested stare.

"Gambler, tall, thick Creole accent, goes by the name of 'River'."

"I've seen him around. He comes in here sometimes, but he usually hangs out over at the Aces and Deuces saloon. A little farther down the street on your right."

Cord tossed the shot and replaced the empty glass and then fished out two coins, dropping them onto the bar. "Thanks."

The bartender nodded as he picked up the change with his burly fingers, watching Cord leave his establishment and walk over to his horse. Cord took the buckskin's reins and began walking it down the street while making sure to keep an eye out for anything, or anyone, suspicious. Before he had made it to the Aces and Deuces he passed the sheriff's office, but decided to forgo announcing his arrival nor his intent. Besides Sheriff Sage Connelly and Deputy Tom Wills he had no way of knowing who had befriended River and he wasn't willing to take the chances of finding out the hard way.

As he stepped up to the front of the saloon, he could feel the anticipation building within him. It had been a long time coming, almost a year, to get the notice that River had been spotted. After loosely tying off the buckskin he wondered how much resistance the man would put up to the notion of being brought in. Knowing that he would be facing murder charges Cord imagined that he probably wouldn't be willing to go very easily.

He stepped up to the batwing doors and paused, drawing in a deep breath before pushing open the doors and stepping in, immediately taking a short step off to the side to minimize the outline of his arrival against the bright afternoon sun. His eyes adjusted as he scanned the room which was speckled with patrons, some of which were lining the bar while others congregated at various tables. The piano player was pounding out a lively song on an old upright, an occasional sour note ringing out and making itself obvious, but still going unnoticed by the inattentive crowd. Cord's eyes were panning those inside the saloon when he saw a card game going on at a table in the far back of the elongated room. He searched the faces of each man, a feat not easily accomplished due to the dimmed lighting and the considerable distance to the back. He saw the dealer wearing a black Stetson sitting among the players, but because of the darkened view he was still not completely sure of the man's identity until he heard the man speak. *He would know that voice anywhere. It was the voice of River Holloway.*

Cord removed the trigger guard and loosened his Colt in the holster without taking his eyes off of River. He wanted to walk over to the man, pull his gun and shoot him down just like he had done to Billy Richmond. He wanted it so badly he could taste it, but he suppressed those emotions as he kept telling himself that there was nothing that would be gained by such an action. He pushed back the urge and slowly walked over towards the table. Before he had made it over to it, one of the men sitting in the game with his side to Cord caught a glimpse of Cord out of the corner of his eye and looked up. His surprised look was overcome with concern as if knowing what was about to transpire and causing him to suddenly throw down his hand and stand and take a few steps back from the table, all without breaking eye contact with Cord.

River Holloway had been in the middle of dealing out cards when he glanced up and saw Cord stepping up just outside the funneled glare of the overhead lantern hanging low above the table. When their eyes locked, he slowly placed the deck onto the table and cautiously removed the thin, brown cigar hanging from his lips, carefully placing it in the ashtray sitting off to the side as the remaining two players quickly stood and pushed back from the table and all but disappeared into the recesses of the darkened room. River's face was mostly concealed by the black Stetson, but Cord could still make out his beady eyes from underneath the brim and the arrogant smile that had characteristically formed on his face.

"Well, well, well, if it isn't my old acquaintance, Cord Chantry," River announced loud enough for everyone in the tranquil saloon to hear. "How do you do, sir?"

"Alright, River, let's go," Cord said as he looked at him through hard, level eyes.

"And may I ask where we will be embarking?"

"I'm taking you over to the jail."

"Oh, I apologize for disrupting your plans, old friend, but I'm afraid that will not work for me."

"I don't care whether or not it works for you, you're going regardless. And don't call me your 'friend'."

"Why, Cord, your words hurt me to my very core. Regardless, might I inquire as to the reason behind this endeavor?"

"Because you deserve to go there."

"Why, whatever do you mean, sir?"

"You know why. You killed Billy Richmond in cold blood."

"I beg to differ, my good man, but need I remind you that Mr. Richmond pulled a gun on me."

"He was nothing but a young kid."

"Have it your way, sir. Then he was a young kid who pulled a gun on me."

"He pulled his gun because you had a gun covering us."

"That is not the sequence of events as I recall them to be so I'm afraid it comes down to my word against yours."

"I'm not going to argue with you, River. I want you to get up and come with me. *Now.*"

"And what shall your response be if I should decline your demands?"

"You don't want to find out."

River slowly sat back in his chair, allowing room for his right hand to casually slide down under the table. "Why, Mr.

Chantry, I do believe that sounds like a threat. Are you, in fact, threatening me, sir? Because everyone in this saloon is listening to this exchange."

Cord watched the movement of River's hand very carefully before glancing around the room. Everyone there was staring at him, silently judging him and anxiously awaiting to see the outcome. He felt at a disadvantage since he didn't know how proficient River was with a gun and being in a somewhat crowded, darkened saloon wasn't the place he wanted to find out. He needed to get him out of there without being forced to draw his gun. He had to push him harder.

"River, you aren't going to talk your way out of this so you might as well stop trying. You're coming with me one way or another so stop stalling. It isn't going to work."

"And again, Mr. Chantry, just what is the alternative, might I ask? Are you willing to gun me down right here in this establishment in front of all of these people? Is that your intention, sir?"

"I'm not leaving here without you, River, so get up now."

"Or what?" River responded cooly, his arrogance leaking through his contemptuous smirk.

Cord stood quietly as doubt began to flood his mind. This wasn't going like he had hoped it would. He knew what River was doing. He was building a case, trying to make himself look like the victim so if things suddenly went south he could claim Cord was bullying and threatening him and he would have all of the people in the saloon to verify his side of the story. He was trying to force Cord to lose his patience and make a mistake, to make the first move so that way he would be justified in whatever actions he, River, took to defend himself. It was the perfect setup.

"River, I'm not going to ask you again," Cord stated boldly as he fought back his building anger and impatience.

"Get up." He tried to watch River's right arm for movement. Since River was an expert at maintaining his composure it was impossible to say if he were stalling or if he was just waiting for the right moment to fire. Cord couldn't tell whether or not River had already drawn his gun. The sly grin of confidence on his face led Cord to believe he had.

Cord had had enough. He had to make a move before he lost his temper anymore. "If you won't come on your own, I guess I'll have to drag you over there."

The comment was just what River was looking for. As soon as Cord said it, he kept his eye on River's right hand knowing the comment would spark him to make a move. He saw River's shoulder raise slightly as he moved his hidden gun and took aim under the table. The move was very subtle, but Cord had seen enough shots fired from concealment that he knew what to look for. Cord drew his weapon and fired.

River thought he had the element of surprise, but he didn't count on Cord's speed. The shot pierced River's white ruffled Bard shirt producing a gushing well of blood just above the top button of his black Frock coat. River's face suddenly flashed with surprise as his eyes widened and his mouth fell open. His expression never changed as his body slowly fell forward until his face landed on the table, his right hand dropping out of his lap and down by his side as the gun, a pearl-handle Colt Paterson revolver he had been holding slipped from his grip and dropped onto the floor with a thud. Cord holstered his smoking Colt and stared at the dead man as he heard footsteps running across the wooden floor and out of the saloon, no doubt of someone going to alert Sheriff Connelly.

One of the men who had been playing cards with River walked back over to the table and felt the side of River's neck, although his condition was obvious to everyone. After several seconds, the man removed his fingers and looked firmly over at Cord. "He's dead." A second man from the bar, a curious young man wearing a black Hardee hat had walked over to the table and bent over to pick up River's gun as he looked down at River's body and then glanced over at Cord. "You killed him."

CHAPTER FIVE

"I can't say as I'm sad to hear that," Cord spoke calmly to the first man who had verified River's passing. "He had it coming."

Cord heard the batwing doors opening behind him, followed by several sets of footsteps coming inside. "What's going on in here?" Sheriff Connelly asked as he and Deputy Tom Wills continued walking farther into the saloon. The two men stopped alongside Cord, staring at River's body slumped over the table. Cord didn't offer an explanation since he knew the answer was evident. "Oh no, Cord, what did you do?"

"I didn't have a choice," Cord answered.

"You shot that man," one of the men at the bar responded.

"Yeah," another voice added. "He didn't want to go with him, but you kept pushing him to."

"He tried to tell you he wasn't going with you, but you wouldn't leave him alone," yet another stated.

Sheriff Connelly looked over at the bartender. "Mel, what happened here?"

Cord looked at the bartender who seemed reluctant to answer with Cord staring at him, but he swallowed hard and looked at the sheriff. "That fella was sitting there playing cards, minding his own business," he stated as he pointed first at River and then at Cord, "and then *he* came in and started threatening him and when that gambler wouldn't go with him he shot him."

"That's not what happened," Cord said defensively. He turned and looked at Sheriff Connelly. "That's not what happened at all, Sage."

Sheriff Connelly's eyes went hard. "Cord, I warned you not to take the law into your own hands."

Cord was shocked by what he was hearing. "I didn't, Sage. I came in here to bring him over to you."

"But I told you to leave it alone."

"But he killed my friend."

"And now you've killed him. It doesn't work that way. This is not 'an eye for an eye'. I told you to leave it alone. You should have waited until we could get the federal marshall out here."

"And by then he would have probably been gone."

"Maybe, but at least he would still be alive and you wouldn't be facing charges."

The words caught Cord's attention. "*Charges?* You can't be serious?"

"I'm afraid I am, Cord," Sheriff Connelly stated flatly. "You give me no choice. Give me your gun," he added as he held out his hand. "I need you to come with me."

Cord couldn't believe what he was hearing. "Sage, I don't understand this. You're actually going to arrest me for killing a murderer?"

"He hadn't even been accused of murder. You don't give me any choice. I have to. It's my job."

Cord looked into his friend's eyes. He could tell the decision was wracking him with guilt, but he understood what he had to do. If he wasn't able to take a man into custody with his deputy standing right next to him then everyone he came across would challenge him and he would quickly lose control over the town. In no time at all, his reputation and his career would be over, or worse, he would wind up dead. As satisfying as it felt to know that River Holloway was dead it still wasn't enough satisfaction to ruin another man's life, especially when he was only doing his job, a job that he was sworn to do. Cord sighed and slowly reached into his holster and handed his Colt over to Sheriff Connelly.

"Tom," Sheriff Connelly said, "go get Paul. Tell him there's a body in here for him."

Deputy Wills nodded and walked out of the saloon as Sheriff Connelly turned back to Cord. "Okay, Cord. Let's go."

Cord took one last quick look around the patrons in the saloon, their faces telling him everything without the need for words. He could see from their expressions that no one was going to be on his side in this. He walked past Sheriff Connelly and out the door over to the sheriff's office. When both men were inside, the sheriff spoke. "Hold up, Cord."

Cord stood still as the sheriff retrieved the keys from his desk drawer and closed it. "Alright." He walked him into the back room where the cells were and Cord stepped into the first one with the door standing open. He made it to the middle of the small cage and turned around to face Connelly, a mixed look of defeat and betrayal covering his face. Connelly chose not to make eye contact with Cord until after he had swung the heavy metal door shut and locked it. Only then could he finally mister up the nerve to look him in the eye. "I'm sorry, Cord, I really am. For what it's worth, I understand why you did what you did."

Cord gave him a unsatisfying look as he held his hands out to emphasize his surroundings. "But yet, here I am."

"I'm sorry, Cord, but I tried to warn you not to go after River and you did it anyway. I had no choice. You've gotta understand that. Look at it from my point of view."

"I don't expect you to make an exception for me just because we're friends, Sage, but knowing what you know about me and what you've heard about River I also didn't expect you to take his side."

"River's dead," Sheriff Connelly pointed out flatly. "He no longer has a side."

A knock at the door interrupted Judge Hess from looking over some briefs on an upcoming trial that he would be presiding over. The disruption caused him to sigh heavily, his irritation clearly visible as he looked up from the documents at the door to see who was causing him grief. "Come in," he reluctantly invited them in. The door opened and a wiry man stuck his head in and waited for the judge to respond to his presence. "Yes, Leonard. I don't know what you need, but this had better be good," the judge warned him as he sighed heavily again. "What can I do for you?" he asked insincerely.

"Sorry to bother you, your honor," the man nervously fumbled with his words as he adjusted his wire rimmed glasses on his face, "but you told me to let you know if there was ever any serious crimes committed inside the town limits."

"Well what it it?" Judge Hess asked, still not convinced that the answer would be worth the interruption.

"A man's been killed in one of the saloons."

The news immediately peaked Judge Hess' interest as he laid down the papers he had been holding. "Who was it? What happened?"

"I'm not really sure, your honor. I only know that a man was killed."

"Well, get someone in here who *does* know," the judge demanded. "I can't work off of tiny bits of information, Leonard. That doesn't do me any good. I need to know the whole story. Now get me someone who can tell me the whole story."

"Yessir. Right away, sir," Leonard Baker acknowledged as he nodded quickly and ducked back behind the door, closing it behind him. He grabbed his hat and went out the office door briskly walking in the direction of the sheriff's office. Once he had arrived, he entered through the door and saw Sheriff Connelly standing next to the potbellied stove across the room pouring himself a cup of coffee. Connelly looked up to see who was coming in to see him.

"Sheriff, I need you to come with me," Leonard Baker blurted out without a greeting.

"Well, hello to you, too, Leonard. What do you mean I need to come with you?"

"Judge Hess wants to see you right now. It's about the shooting."

Sheriff Connelly replaced the old metal coffee pot back onto the burner of the stove and walked back over to his desk as he gingerly brought the cup to his lips and squinted as he took a dangerous sip. The heat caught him by surprise even though he had expected it. "Why does he have to know right now? Why can't this wait until the next time I'm over his way?"

"I don't know, sheriff, but I do know that he gave me explicit instructions to bring you back over to his office right away. Now, are you coming or should I tell him that you're unwilling?"

Sheriff Connelly took another careful sip before setting down the cup onto his desk. "Okay, fine. I'll go now," he reluctantly announced.

"Thank you, sheriff," Leonard Baker responded with a

smirky smile before turning and walking out the door, his head held a little higher that he had succeeded in his task.

Sage Connelly watched the wormy man leave, agitated that he was being summoned by Judge Hess. He had never liked the man, regardless of the fact that he stood for the law. Sage had always questioned whether or not the judge was clean, especially since certain things had happened in the past to suggest otherwise, but there had never been enough evidence to prove anything substantial. Still, he didn't trust the man nor did he agree with his tactics. The man was ruthless and nothing was more dangerous than a ruthless man with power.

Sheriff Connelly made the short trip over to the judge's chambers and showed his presence to Leonard Baker who was sitting at his desk outside in the next room. Leonard briefly disappeared into the judge's chamber and then reappeared with his smirky fake smile. "Judge Hess will see you now."

Sheriff Connelly walked through the door that Leonard had opened for him and waited for the judge to direct him.

"Ah, Sheriff Connelly. Please, have a seat," Judge Hess motioned with his hand as Sage took the seat directly in front of his large desk.

"Leonard said you wanted to see me?"

"Yes, sheriff," Judge Hess replied as he leaned his meaty arms on the desk. "I heard that a man was killed here in town, is that right?"

"Yessir, that's right."

"Did you apprehend the killer?"

Sheriff Connelly didn't approve of the use of the label, but decided to forgo pointing it out to the judge in a disagreement. "Yessir. He's already in custody."

"Good, good, "Judge Hess proclaimed happily as he leaned back in his chair and casually ran his hand over his balding head. "One thing we always need to make sure of in this town, sheriff, is that we keep the riffraff under control. I hope he didn't put up too much resistance to being arrested?"

"No, sir. He wasn't any trouble at all."

"Good, good," Judge Hess repeated. "So what do you know about this incident?"

"The man who was shot was a gambler that had only been in town a week or two. His name was River Hammond. The man who shot him is a cowhand from Benton Springs."

Judge Hess repositioned himself in his leather chair. "Benton Springs? What's he doing over here?"

"He has friends here," Sheriff Connelly explained without offering the fact that he happened to be one of them.

"And the killer's name?"

"Cord Chantry."

"Chantry...Chantry..." Judge Hess repeated as he scribbled the name down on an available piece of paper. "Never heard of him. Is he wanted anywhere?"

"I don't think so, your honor."

"Leonard said this shooting took place in one of our saloons. Were there any witnesses?"

"Yessir. Maybe a dozen or so."

"Good. That'll make the trial go that much smoother."

"Yessir."

"Well, that's mighty good work, sheriff. We wouldn't want the good people of Hurley to think we were going to allow their safety or their quality of life to be jeopardized by some low-life saddle trash with no regard for others. I won't tolerate it. Now all we have to do is make an example out of this killer and it will deter others of his kind from tarnishing the reputation of this fine, peaceful little town. There hasn't been a killing in this town since I arrived and I'll be damned if they're going to start now. I'll put an end to this right now."

Sage Connelly knew what the judge meant by the statement. It wasn't the town's reputation that he was worried about, it was his own. "Your honor, this man isn't as dangerous as you might be led to believe because of his actions. He just got caught up in circumstances and made a bad choice, that's all."

"There's no need to side with this kind of trash, sheriff. I take great care to keep this town safe and I won't stand for someone breaking the law, no matter how wonderful of a person you think they are. That's why we need to make an example of this fella."

Hearing the statement for the second time was starting to stir concern within Sheriff Connelly. "May I ask your honor how you plan on doing that?"

Jude Hess' expression turned stern as a frown gathered between his eyes. "We need to have a trial as quickly as possible. Make an example of this man. That's why I need you to gather as much information as you can, as quickly as you can. We need to get on this and strike while the iron is hot."

"Yessir."

"We have to convince the people of Hurley that we aren't going to put up with this type of lawlessness in this town. A hanging is just the thing to do that."

The comment caught Sheriff Connelly by surprise. "A *hanging?* Are you sure that we should jump to that conclusion right away, sir?"

"It sounds like a open-and-shut case to me, sheriff. A drifter comes into town, has a run-in with one of the newcomers to our town and he kills him in front of a room full of witnesses. Exactly what kind of conclusion am I jumping to?"

"Your honor, we don't know all of the facts just yet," Sheriff Connelly pointed out. "Maybe this Chantry fella didn't have a choice. Maybe the gambler provoked him in some way."

"Well, it's up to you to find that out, now isn't it, sheriff?"

"Yessir. I'll get right on it."

"You do that, sheriff," Judge Hess said flatly, but still smiling. "And keep me posted, alright?"

Sheriff Connelly forced a smile as he stood and put on his hat to leave. "Yessir."

CHAPTER SIX

The walk back to the jail was longer than Sage Connelly had
ever remembered it being before. He dreaded the thought of
telling Cord what Judge Hess had just said to him. There was
just no good way to put it. Judge Hess clearly had an agenda
and unfortunately Cord was going to be the first example of
that agenda. It did not look good.

Sheriff Connelly walked into his office and tossed his hat
onto the desk before walking straight in the back to Cord's
cell. Cord was lying on his back quietly staring up at the dull
ceiling. When he saw Sage coming in he sat up and then
stood, walking over and casually grabbing the bars that separated them to hear what he had to say. He immediately
noticed that Connelly wasn't doing a good job of hiding his
concern.

"You don't have to be a genius to know that's not a good
look," Cord surmised with a frown.

"I just had a discussion with Judge Hess," Sage started and
then briefly hesitated. "He's the new judge for the territory
and he's power hungry. He says he wants to make an example
out of you."

Cord flashed his friend a confused look. "What does *that* mean?"

"It means he's not going to go easy on you. He isn't willing to be lenient at all," Sage added and then paused again before looking at him grimly, not wanting to say the words. "He's already talking about a hanging."

"*What?* Are you *kidding me?* It was self-defense."

"*I* know that and *you* know that, but Judge Hess doesn't care. He's only interested in prosecuting you as quickly as possible."

"Prosecute me? Sage, there hasn't even been a trial."

"I know."

"Is there any chance he'll change his mind?"

"I don't see it happening. He's on this power kick and he's not going to back down."

Cord stared past Sheriff Connelly's face and off into the distance. He couldn't believe what he was hearing. He was at a loss for words.

"If you had just listened to me and left River alone none of this would be happening right now and you wouldn't be in there facing a trial," Sage blurted out as his only defense. "I told you to leave him alone. Why couldn't you just ride out of town and leave him be?"

"He deserved to die, Sage."

"Did he? Was it worth *this?*"

"Do you want me to say I regret it because I won't. I don't regret it. I'm not sorry he's dead, Sage. I didn't want to kill him, but he drew on me. I didn't have a choice."

"You had a choice, Cord," Sage snapped harshly out of nowhere. "You had plenty of choices and you blew them, all of them. You had the choice to leave town without confronting him. You had a choice of waiting for the federal marshall. You had a choice of not pulling your gun. Why wouldn't you just listen?" Sheriff Connelly took in a deep breath and tried to calm his emotions back down from the outburst. A few tense seconds passed before Cord spoke first.

"What about the witnesses? There were witnesses there that saw exactly what happened."

Sheriff Connelly shook his head. "That's no good. They won't side with you. Everyone's scared of this new judge. He's already put the fear in every cowboy and drifter in town."

Cord gave Sage a defeated look. "So, that's it? I get to hang for defending myself?"

"I don't know what to say, Cord. There's not a whole lot I can do here. Y'know, you didn't leave me with very many options."

Cord slowly stepped back from the bars and sat back down on the edge of his bed. "Well, I guess it's a good thing I didn't propose to Madeline."

The comment brought Sheriff Connelly back around, a look of surprise on his face. "Wait...*what?* You were going to propose to Madeline?"

"Yeah," Cord nodded slightly, his voice soft and defeated. "I planned on doing it when I got back to Benton Springs. I was going to take her out on a picnic and do it then."

Sheriff Connelly felt his insides being torn out. Despite how much he knew Cord hated River, he knew he was telling him the truth about the shooting being self-defense, but regardless of that it still didn't look like it was going to be enough to save Cord from a hangman's noose.

Sage Connelly walked back into his office and sat at his desk staring off into the room at nothing in particular while pondering the situation with Cord. He had never imagined that things would have come to this, but here they were. Sure, he expected Cord to catch up to River eventually, but his hopes were that it would have taken place somewhere outside of the city limits, out of sight and away from any witnesses, preferably when he was unaware of it until after it had been handled. The worst thing that could have happened had actually happened and now he was going to have to watch his friend suffer the consequences of his actions.

Sage kept running Judge Hess' reaction over in his mind. The comments he had heard the man make were troublesome, but again, there was nothing he could do about it. He had hoped to reason with the judge and hold Cord until the federal marshall made it to town, but Judge Hess didn't seem to be interested in sharing that sentiment and waiting that long. He was in a hurry to prosecute Cord and be done with it and there was nothing Sheriff Connelly could do to stop him. Judge Hess seemed to be in a hurry to deal with Cord, but Connelly didn't understand why. With Cord in jail it wasn't like he was going anywhere. If it took the federal marshall a month to make it to Hurley, which was far longer than it actually should take him then what was the problem with that? What difference would it make? In the meantime it could possibly save a man's life. Wasn't that certainly worth the wait? Connelly thought so but he would never be able to convince Judge Hess of such.

Sage thought about going back over to the judge's chambers and trying to plead Cord's case, but something was stopping him. If he pushed Cord's innocence too much Judge Hess would most certainly become suspicious of his interest in things. Sooner or later it would come out that Cord was a friend of his. That could actually work against Cord because then Judge Hess would know that Sage had a private stake in things and he could, and most likely would, remove Cord from Sage's custody, placing him elsewhere and then Cord wouldn't have anyone on his side. Not only that but it could also very easily escalate a hanging. As he continued running the situation over in his mind Sheriff Connelly heard approaching footsteps and looked over just as Deputy Tom Wills walked through the door.

"Hey, sheriff," the deputy announced as he checked to make sure the door to the back room where the cells were located was closed. "How's Cord?" he asked while trying to keep his voice down.

"Not good," Sheriff Connelly responded. "He's pretty down about things. I can't say as I blame him."

Deputy Wills took the seat across from the desk. "What did Judge Hess have to say?"

"He's already pushing for a hanging."

"*What?* Why is he in such a hurry?"

"I don't now. I think there's an ulterior motive in there somewhere. He just hasn't admitted what it is."

"Does Cord know?"

"Yeah, I felt like I had to let him know what was going on."

"How did he take it?"

"How would *you* take it? He feels like everything and everyone is against him. He thinks he's being railroaded."

"Maybe we should go talk to the ones that were in the saloon and get their side of things."

Sage shook his head, obviously disturbed. "That could work against us. If they have a different opinion of the circumstances things could blow up in our faces and that would only go towards proving Judge Hess right and making matters worse for Cord."

"What else are you going to do, sheriff? If you don't do that then it doesn't leave you with a whole lot of options."

Sheriff Connelly weighed the risk of talking to the people in the saloon and decided there wasn't much more damage it could do to Cord's case at this point. In fact, they might actually even get lucky and find someone who could collaborate Cord's side of things. It was worth a try.

"I'm going to head over to the saloon and talk to some people," Sheriff Connelly announced as he stood and grabbed his hat. "I'll be back in a little while."

"Okay, sheriff," Deputy Wills responded as he watched the sheriff leaving before pouring himself a cup of coffee.

Sheriff Connelly headed straight for the saloon hoping that at least some of the original people who witnessed the shooting were still in there. As he parted the swinging doors he glanced around at those present, looking for familiar faces. He tried to recall who he had seen in there before but he wasn't quite sure about most of them. He decided to do it the easy way.

"Could I have your attention?" he announced as the murmuring in the room began to dissipate until it was completely quiet. "Did anyone see the shooting in here earlier?" The sheriff looked around at the men's faces, all of whom remained silent. Either no one was aware, they weren't present when it had happened or else they were too afraid to get involved. Something told him it was probably the latter. Discouraged by the lack of support, Sage succumbed to the silence and walked over to the bar where the bartender was busy cleaning the counter.

"Mel, did you actually see the shooting?" Sheriff Connelly asked.

"Kind of, sheriff" the bartender, Mel, replied. "It was kind of hard to see everything because there were people standing in the way, but I did hear what went on."

"What did you hear?"

"That gambler was playing cards at the back table. The drifter came in and said he was taking him over to your office, but the gambler said he wasn't going. The next thing I knew, the drifter shot him."

"Did they argue?"

"No, the gambler was as calm as he could be. So was the drifter. They just didn't agree with one another."

"How many shots were there?"

"Just the one."

The answer struck Connelly as being odd. "Wait...the gambler didn't shoot?"

The bartender, Mel, thought for a brief second before he answered. "No...there was just the one shot."

"So you're saying the gambler didn't get off a shot?"

"He couldn't. He didn't have a gun."

"The gambler wasn't armed? The drifter shot an unarmed man?"

"He must have because I only heard the one shot."

Sheriff Connelly was troubled by the statement. Now, that changed everything. He had not expected Cord to kill River in cold blood. He had hated the man, that wasn't a secret, but to kill him when he was unarmed? He thought he knew Cord better than that, thought he had judged him correctly and had a good sense of the man's integrity and honor, but perhaps he had misjudged him after all. Maybe he wanted to believe in Cord so much that he let his perception of him become tainted. Maybe Cord was just putting on a front just waiting for the opportunity to get close enough to River to gun him down. It looked as if he had made a mistake in admitting what Cord was capable of and it had cost River Holloway his life. His failure made him sick.

"Is there anything else, sheriff?" Mel asked.

Sheriff Connelly was beside himself with guilt. "No...no, Mel, that's all. I appreciate it." He turned back to the others in the room. "Did anyone see the gambler draw a weapon?" He looked around the room at their faces as he waited for no one to respond. He had his answer.

Mel threw Sheriff Connelly a grin and turned to get back

to work as Sheriff Connelly pondered his next move. He couldn't get over how wrong he had been about Cord. It was eating him up that he would have to live with his mistake for the rest of his life. Even worse was knowing that because of him River Holloway would not get that chance.

CHAPTER SEVEN

A defeated Sheriff Connelly walked back over to his office as he contemplated what he was going to say to Cord Chantry. The man had clearly deceived him and taken him and his trust for granted, which angered him to his very core. He, Sage, had made mistakes before during his tenure in maintaining the law but it was nothing of this magnitude. He had never outright shot a man who couldn't defend himself. There was no explanation that Cord could give him that could ever make that acceptable.

Even though he was the sheriff his carelessness had caused a man to be killed, plain and simple. The mistake made him begin to question if he was even fit to keep his position. Once word spread to the townspeople they would question it, too, and maybe they were correct to do so. If he wasn't capable of protecting one individual from being gunned down in a public place in front of witnesses, no matter how despicable that individual might have been, then maybe he had lost his touch and should step down from his position as sheriff before someone else needlessly lost their life.

When Sheriff Connelly walked into his office Deputy

Tom Wills was sitting behind the desk with his feet casually perched atop it. Surprised when the sheriff walked in, Deputy Wills quickly swung his feet down in embarrassment hoping the sheriff wouldn't call him on it, but realizing that he was still too late in his reaction to hide it. He tried to question the sheriff to divert his actions.

"What did they say, sheriff?" he asked innocently.

Sheriff Connelly walked right past Deputy Wills and into the back room with the cells. His ignoring Deputy Will's question was not intentional, but rather because Sage was too wrapped up in getting answers from Cord to respond to his deputy. When he stopped in front of Cord's cell, Cord was lying on his back on his bunk. When he saw that it was Sheriff Connelly he got up and walked over to the bars, a simple smile on his face. "Sage, what brings you back here?" he asked innocently.

Sage dismissed the pleasantries. "I just got back from talking to the men in the saloon," he replied, his tone dirty without any type of emotion. "They're in agreement that River was shot down."

Cord looked shocked by the information. "What do you mean? What did they say?"

"I could only find one person who would talk about it. The bartender. He said that there was only one shot. Yours."

"They think I shot an unarmed man?" Cord asked, more as a statement than a question. Then, the realization of what the sheriff was saying hit him. "*You* think I shot an unarmed man?"

Sage shook his head, obviously disturbed. "I don't know what to think, Cord. I want to believe you, but the evidence doesn't look good."

"Why? Just because of one man's opinion?"

"It wasn't just an opinion, Cord, it was his statement. He didn't hear another shot."

"That's because River didn't get off a shot. I killed him before he had a chance to."

"Well, because of that it doesn't look good for you."

"So it's my fault that I didn't let River shoot me?"

"I'm not saying that. I'm saying there are no other witnesses to collaborate your story."

"What about River's gun? Shouldn't *that* be enough to collaborate my story?"

"*What* gun? River didn't have a gun."

Cord's look of surprised wasn't lost on Sheriff Connelly. "Yes, he did. It was a pearl-handled Colt Paterson. I saw it with my own two eyes."

The news caught Sage off-guard. If Cord were lying to him he was going to a lot of trouble and being very specific to do so. "You're saying you actually saw him with a gun?"

Cord nodded. "That's exactly what I'm saying. How else would I know what he was carrying?"

Cord had a point. But was it enough to convince the right people of his innocence?

"That doesn't make sense," Sage pointed out, his tone calm, but confused. "If River did have a gun, then where is it?"

"I don't know."

"Tell me exactly what happened."

"I walked into the saloon looking for River. At first, I didn't see him, but then I spotted him at the very back table facing the door playing cards with three other men. Initially, when I walked up to the table, one of the men got up and stepped back out of the way. Then the other two moved back and it was just me and River."

"And then?"

"I told River I was bringing him into your office and he refused. His hand was under the table and I saw him go for his gun."

"You saw the gun under the table?"

"No, but I could tell it was there."

"You mean you saw him reaching for it?"

"Yeah."

"Then what happened?"

"I shot him."

Sheriff Connelly was confused by Cord's recollection of the events. "But if he had a gun, why didn't we find it?"

"I don't know why because I saw it..."

Cord's words abruptly stopped as his face was masked in shock as if he suddenly remembered something of considerable importance. "The kid," he stated in a softer tone.

"What kid?" Sage asked curiously.

Cord recalled the rest of what had happened. "One of the men playing cards with River walked over and checked his neck to see if he was alive, but there was also someone else, a young kid. Well, not an actual kid, but he was certainly younger than me. Maybe twenty or so, at the most."

"What about him?"

Cord stared off into the air while he spoke as if he were recalling the events of the scene. "He reached down and picked up the gun and then he said, 'you killed him'."

"Then what?"

The question snapped Cord back to the present as he stared back at Sage. "That was it. I never saw the gun again after that because I was paying too much attention to River sitting there at the table dead."

"Did this kid walk away? Did he hang around the saloon? What happened to him?"

Cord paused briefly as he tried to remember. "I don't know. That was when you came in. I was too focused on that. By the way, how did you find out what had happened so fast?"

"One of the people in the saloon ran over and got me."

"Was it a young kid?"

"No. It was one of the townspeople that I knew."

"Well, I don't know where he went after that."

"What did this kid look like?"

"He had a baby face, average height, brown hair, tan trousers, dark blue shirt and a tan vest and he was wearing a black Hardee hat."

Sheriff Connelly took in the description as he tried to match it to someone he would know from the townspeople, but he couldn't. "You're saying this young kid took the gun?"

"I'm saying he had to have," Cord insisted. "It's the only thing that makes sense. Where else would it have gone?"

"Then I need to find this kid. It sounds like he's the only one who can clear you."

"If you don't recognize him by a description then what if he's a drifter? He might not even still be in town. What am I going to do if he isn't?"

"Let's not worry about that bridge until we cross it," Sheriff Connelly proposed. "First things first. Right now, I need to look around town and find that kid." Sage gave a simple wave to Cord and walked back out into the sheriff's office where Deputy Wills was still sitting behind the desk. He started to stand when Sage walked in.

"No, you can stay there," Sage assured him. "I need to go do something."

"Do you need my help?" Deputy Wills offered.

"No, I don't think so," Sage initially responded as he started walking towards the door, but then he stopped and turned back to Wills. "On second thought, yeah, I could use the extra set of legs. I need you to help me find someone."

Deputy Wills grabbed his hat and put it on. "Who?"

"A young kid, about twenty, brown hair, average height. He was wearing a dark blue shirt, tan pants and vest and a black Hardee hat."

"Why are we looking for him?"

"He's a witness to a killing."

Both Sheriff Connelly and Deputy Wills left the office, each heading in specific directions with Sheriff Connelly checking out the livery stables while Deputy Wills tried the three hotels in town. When Sage spoke to the stable owner he recalled seeing a young man fitting the description and remembered that the man's horse was a tan mustang. According to the stable owner, the young man had left a few hours earlier, exactly where he was going he wasn't sure.

Deputy Wills had more luck at the second hotel he visited. The clerk there remembered the young man's name and that he checked out after being in town for a couple of days. In a chance conversation they had had when the man was checking out he didn't happen to mention where he was heading although the clerk did mention that he noticed seeing him heading west. As soon as Deputy Wills heard the news he went straight back to the sheriff's office and found Sheriff Connelly sitting behind his desk waiting to hear if Wills had any luck with his search.

"I found out more about him from one of the hotel clerks," Deputy Wills announced as he walked through the sheriff's office door. "His name is Jesse Morse. He didn't know where he was going, but he did say when he left town he was heading west"

"How long ago did he leave?"

"The clerk said somewhere around a couple of hours."

"Is he riding alone?"

"Yeah, as far as he knew. Said he was on a tan mustang with a large white patch on its right side."

Sheriff Connelly took in the information while he quietly pondered his next move. The kid was the only one who could verify Cord's story and exonerate him, but even so it wasn't quite that simple. Besides the fact that he had no idea where the kid was headed there was still another problem. What if the kid didn't still have the gun? What if he had gotten rid of it or sold it? If he was out on his own surely he had a gun of his own, any lone drifter most likely would for protection, if nothing else. Even if he did have it then he, Connelly, would have to be able to convince the kid to come back to Hurley and testify on Cord's behalf and even if he did there was still no guarantee that he would tell the truth even if he did manage to bring him back. And all of that was based on the assumption that he could even find him.

"What's the next move, sheriff?" Deputy Wills asked curiously.

"I'm not sure," Sage said, then hesitated. "I can't just go riding out of town with no plan on where I need to go. That would waste a lot of time and right now time is something Cord doesn't have a lot of." He sat and tried to think through the situation, but he had to admit to himself that there was no easy answer. Finally, he resolved to the obvious conclusion. He would have to go back and try to talk to Judge Hess.

"Stay here, Tom. I need to go see the judge."

Sheriff Connelly grabbed his hat and proceeded out the door and over to the judge's chambers, rolling Cord's case over in his mind as he walked. He didn't expect empathy from the judge, that would be unrealistic to expect, nor did he believe the judge would be willing to offer him any type of assistance or concessions, but if nothing else he needed to get the judge to hold off on his plans to prosecute Cord. If he went to trial now, there would be no way he would come out of this alive. Judge Hess had made that abundantly clear. Sage had to stop the progression of things or, at the very least, slow them down as much as possible until he could come up with some answers.

CHAPTER EIGHT

When Sheriff Connelly entered the clerk's office of Judge
Hess, Leonard was sitting behind his desk in usual fashion
pouring over books with his spectacles hanging down towards
the end of his nose. He looked up when Sheriff Connelly
came through the door.

"Ah, Sheriff Connelly," Leonard stated in a disingenuous
tone. "What brings you back so quickly?"

"Is Judge Hess in?"

"He is, but I'm not sure he can see you right now, sheriff,"
Leonard responded, the sarcasm filling his face and his voice.

Sage's expression made it clear that he was not in the
mood for such games. "Leonard, this can't wait. It's about a
situation I talked to the judge about earlier so just tell me, is
he in or not?"

Leonard shot the sheriff a disgruntled look, aggravated
that Connelly had not been sucked into his display of control.
Finally, he conceded. "Yes. I'll go see if he can see you."

"Thanks," Sage said as he retuned the fake smile Leonard
had given him. Leonard was only in the office a few seconds
when he opened the door for the sheriff. "He'll see you now."

Sheriff Connelly walked past Leonard who gave him a pretentious glare as he did. He closed the door behind Sage once he was inside the judge's chambers.

"Sheriff, have a seat," Judge Hess instructed him as he glared at him while he was sitting down. Sage glimpsed the speculation in the man's eyes. The arrogance in the room was thick enough to choke him. It felt unsettling to be sitting in front of the man in his own domain as if he had authority over everyone else in town or even in the entire territory. Connelly believed that was exactly the way Judge Hess had intended it to be. "What can I do for you?"

"I came across some new information about the shooting."

"Oh, and what might that be?" Jude Hess leaned back lazily in his chair with notable disinterest.

"We found a witness that saw the gun owned by the gambler that was shot. It looks as if he picked it up right after the shooting."

The question caught Sheriff Connelly by surprise. "I see. And why would he do that?"

Sage hesitated, unsure if he was asking out of curiosity or if he was trying to point out how ludicrous he thought the notion to be. "I'm...not sure, your honor. Maybe he wanted it as a souvenir?"

Judge Hess did not show enough interest to be impressed. "Uh-huh...and just where is this witness now, sheriff?" he asked while cocking his head to the side, his skepticism clearly visible.

"He left town," Sheriff Connelly reluctantly admitted.

"I see. And how did you come about this information?"

Sheriff Connelly could see the case the judge was building and he didn't like it. "We heard it from the drifter."

"The drifter? The same man who is accused of murdering a man?"

"Yessir."

"Uh-huh. And do you have any other witnesses?"

Sage hesitated. "Uh...no sir."

"In a room full of witnesses no one else saw this alleged man...

There it was.

"...pick up the dead man's gun?"

"Uh..."

"That would be a 'no', sheriff."

"I just need to find this man, your honor, and bring him in so we can clear up this mess."

"How do you even know that there is a man?"

"Because that was the information that we were given."

"By the killer."

"By the *alleged* killer."

As soon as the sheriff said it, he knew he had made a critical mistake. His fears were instantly confirmed when Judge Hess's expression quickly took a dramatic turn for the worst. He clearly didn't appreciate the sheriff correcting him, especially by using a legal term that he didn't think Sheriff Connelly was qualified to use.

"Now, see here sheriff, I'm all for finding out the truth. For heaven's sake, that's my job. I'm sworn to uphold the law, just like you. And like you, I have to follow up on any information that is pertinent to a case. But I don't have to listen to the ramblings of a killer who has been caught red-handed committing a murder in front of a room full of witnesses. I will not tie up valuable resources to send you on a wild goose chase after a man that more than likely doesn't even exist."

"But your honor..."

"I'm telling you right now sheriff that we are not going to waste your time and certainly not mine following up on a lead from the killer himself. It just isn't going to happen. Not on my watch. If this is the only proof you have that there was another witness then you have nothing."

"But your honor..."

"I don't want to hear of it, Connelly, this man is just pulling your leg to drag out this investigation. The fact of the matter is there *is* no witness. If there were, we'd have heard about it before now from someone else, someone credible, that is. This man is just fishing to see if you'll take the bait and I've got to be honest with you, sheriff, I'm surprised that you fell for his deception so easily. I haven't known you for very long, but you seemed like a better and smarter man than that."

"Your honor, please..."

"No, no, now sheriff, we aren't going to discuss this any further. The man is guilty. He killed a man. There were plenty of witnesses that saw him pull the trigger, but there are no witnesses who can substantiate his story that there was another gun. What does that tell you? I don't know about *you,* sheriff, but it tells *me* that the man is guilty, guilty, guilty and he needs to pay for his actions."

"Your honor, the reason no one else saw this man pick up the gambler's gun is because it was dark and it happened so fast. The man who picked it up..."

"*Allegedly* picked it up," Jude Hess quickly corrected him. Connelly knew the correction was a jab at him doing the same thing to Judge Hess earlier.

"...allegedly picked it up was already checking on the gambler. It happened so quick that no one had a chance to realize what he was doing and that he had picked up the gun."

"We're not going to discuss this any longer, sheriff. I need you to do your job and stop chasing fictitious witnesses. Now, if you can't handle doing that then I'll find someone else who can. I hear your deputy is quite a capable young man. Perhaps he can do your job better than you can. If you don't drop this nonsense immediately, I'll be forced to make some adjustments and we'll find out if he can. Is that clear, sheriff?"

Sage was disgusted with the judge's behavior and his seemingly immediate dismissal of the facts. It was as if he, Judge Hess, had already made up his mind about Cord, regardless of the facts being laid out for him. Sage decided to speak his mind even if it came at the cost of his job, which it sounded like Judge Hess was already considering doing, anyway. "I thought a man was innocent until *proven* guilty?"

Judge Hess did not take the insinuation lightly. His eyes did not waiver and his tone was calm, but there was evident hatred in his voice, hated that this small, insignificant sheriff had dared to question him and his authority. Judge Hess leaned forward and clasped his hands together on the desk so tightly that his knuckles began turning white. "Now you listen to me, sheriff. I've had just about all of the insubordination from you that I'm going to take. I want you to march yourself back over to that office of yours and stay put until this thing is over and if you can't or believe you can't do that then I need you to let me know right now and I'll make other arrangements. Is that in any way unclear?"

Sheriff Connelly felt like climbing over his ridiculously large oak desk and choking the life out of him right then and there, but he knew that would do nothing to help Cord. He had to make sure which battle he was willing to fight in at the moment and this clearly wasn't it. "No, sir," he reluctantly agreed. "I understand."

Judge Hess's resolve was evident. "Perfect. Now, good day, sheriff."

Sage took the hint and stood, walking over to the door and opening it. As he passed by Leonard's desk, he saw the smirk on the wiry worm's face, a smirk he would have gladly been willing to knock off of it.

. . .

Once again, a defeated Sheriff Connelly walked back over to his office, his spirits dampened and his focus unsure on what he was going to do. The meeting with Judge Hess had not gone anywhere near as good as he had anticipated it would. The man was clearly not interested in dealing with the facts. Sage didn't know why the judge was so anxious to get Cord on the end of a noose, but he had been very convincing that neither he, Sage, nor Cord would receive any assistance or consideration from the courts. Sheriff Connelly was at his wit's end as to what he was going, or not going, to do next.

As he made it over to his office Deputy Wills was sitting in one of the chairs out front on the boardwalk motioning to passing townspeople. When he saw the dampened expression on the sheriff's face, his own expression quickly took a dive. "What happened, sheriff?" he asked as Sage was passing by him. Connelly motioned with his head for Deputy Wills to come inside with him, which he did. As Wills walked through the door he was surprised to see the sheriff waiting for him to pass by so he could close the door behind him. Deputy Wills waited in front of the sheriff's desk while Sage walked around and sat down behind it. Wills took the opposing chair and was the first to speak.

"What happened, sheriff?" He asked as he saw first hand the beating Sheriff Connelly's spirit had taken from the meeting.

Sage looked directly into Deputy Wills' eyes, his concern evident. "Judge Hess isn't going to allow us to follow up on the witness."

"*What?* How is that possible? *Why? Why* would he do that?"

Connelly shook his head in disgust. "I don't know. I don't know what his reasoning is. He doesn't believe he exists. All he would say is we weren't to pursue this kid who picked up the gun and if I didn't drop the whole thing he was going to replace me."

The statement caught the deputy's attention. "*Replace* you? With *who?*"

Sage looked at Wills. "You."

"*Me?* Sheriff, I don't want your job."

"I know. It was a scare tactic."

"Well, he can forget it. I'll quit before I'll let him get rid of you and put me in your place. I just won't do it."

Sage Connelly held up his hand to try to calm the situation. "Take it easy, Tom. Thank goodness it hasn't come to that...at least, not yet. And hopefully, it won't."

"So what are we going to do about this?" Tom Wills asked.

"*We* aren't going to do anything," Sage reiterated. "I want you to stay out of this. There's no need for both of us to sabotage our careers."

"But sheriff..."

"No, 'but sheriff'. I'm not going to have your job loss on my conscience. Is that clear?"

"Yessir, sheriff, I understand," Wills responded with a defeated expression.

Sage threw him a faint smile. "But for what it's worth, I appreciate the gesture."

Deputy Wills returned the smile, but his gratitude was short-lived as he could tell that Connelly was struggling with the issue at hand. He decided to restructure the question. "So what's the plan?"

Connelly shook his head in dismay. "I don't know. My hands are tied no matter how I approach this."

The two men sat in silence for what seemed like an eternity as both mulled over the facts. It was several minutes later when Sheriff Connelly finally broke the silence. "Tom, I need you to go over to the livery stables."

"Why, what's going on over there, sheriff?"

Sheriff Connelly had a determined look on his face. "I just need you to go over there."

The request was so unusual that Deputy Wills didn't know quite how to react. "Sure thing, sheriff. Why am I going? Is there a problem over there?"

Connelly stood and looked over at Wills with a flat expression, choosing instead to ignore the question entirely. "Please, Tom. Just promise me that you'll go over to the stables."

Deputy Wills was confused, but he trusted Sheriff Connelly enough not to push the issue. Still, he worried about what his friend was going through. He also wished he could do something, anything, to help him. "Sheriff..."

"Tom, please go. Now."

"Okay, sheriff," Deputy Wills reluctantly agreed with a simple nod. Sheriff Connelly forced a faint smile accompanied with an equally convincing nod. "Then I guess if you need me I'll be over at the livery stables."

"Thanks," Sage said as he continued his charade. He watched Wills open the door and look back at him one last time before shutting it behind him as he left. Sheriff Connelly waited until he heard Wills' footsteps fade off down the boardwalk before he opened the drawer to his desk and retrieved the cell door keys. He then opened the door leading back to the cells and headed towards Cord's cell. As he walked up to it, Cord glanced over from his position lying on his bunk. Cord could tell by the man's expression that he had something serious on his mind. "Sage. What's going on?"

Sheriff Connelly unlocked the cell door and opened it wide.

CHAPTER NINE

The gesture caused Cord to sit up and walk over to the door, stopping just inside of it with a confused look as his curiosity took over. "What are you doing?" Cord asked, his surprised look saying it all.

"I spoke to Judge Hess," Sage started. "He isn't going to give you a fair trial, Cord. He's already made up his mind that you're guilty."

Cord was shocked by the admission. "How can he get away with that?"

"He thinks he has the right to do it because he's the judge for the town, actually for the territory."

"He isn't even going to wait for a trial?"

"No, but it wouldn't matter if he did. He's already decided that you're guilty. A trial would just be a formality. Regardless of what happens, he's going to find you guilty. He already told me that himself."

"He *told* you that?" Cord asked, still stunned at the claim.

"Yeah."

Cord pondered the news only briefly before he looked back at Connelly. "So why are you opening my cell door?"

"You're going to escape."

The words hit Cord hard. "I'm *what?*"

"Judge Hess isn't going to listen to reason, Cord. He's going to put you on trial as fast as he can. If he does that he's going to find you guilty and if he does that he's going to hang you. I'm not going to just stand by and let that happen."

"Sage, you can't be serious."

"I am serious. I believe what you told me, I just can't figure out a way to convince Judge Hess that it's the truth. Until I can do that, it isn't safe for you in here. You need to be out of here, out of town. I can only protect you inside this jail cell for so long. After that, it'll be out of my hands."

"I can't just leave town."

"Well, you can't very well stay here, either. If you do, Hess is likely to have the townspeople just walk over here without a moment's notice, pull you out of your cell and lynch you and if they do that there won't be a single thing I can do to stop them. It would turn into a shootout and a lot of innocent people would be hurt just because of the ravings of a lunatic." Cord wanted to argue with the man, but he knew Sage had a point. The townspeople would listen to Judge Hess' directions over those of Sheriff Connelly. They would do the judge's bidding even if they didn't necessarily agree with it because in their eyes they would be upholding the law. They wouldn't care two shakes about a drifter that killed someone. They would be delivering their own type of frontier justice, swift and firm, just the way townspeople liked it. Sage was right. If he wanted any kind of chance at living long enough to clear his name he couldn't do it from inside this cell.

"But what about you?" Cord asked concerned.

"Don't worry about me," Sage assured him. "I'll be fine."

"No, you won't," Cord argued. "They aren't going to take this lightly. This will all fall on you and they'll tear you apart.

They'll take away your job and you'll never be able to work with the law again. No, I won't let you do it. I won't let you do this to yourself."

"I'm not asking for your permission, Cord, and arguing about it isn't going to change anything. I've already made up my mind. This is happening whether you agree with it or not."

Cord stare at his friend, speechless. The man was sacrificing everything he had worked for, everything he believed in just for him. He was killing his career without giving it a second thought. The gesture overwhelmed Cord. He couldn't believe Sage was so willing to give it all up for him. "Thank you," he said genuinely as he extended his hand. The two men shook as Sage spoke.

"The fellas' name that you're looking for is Jesse Morse. You remember what he looked like and what he was wearing?"

"Yeah."

"He left town a few hours ago. According to the hotel clerk he said he was headin' west. That's all I know."

Cord looked at his friend. "Sage, are you sure you want to do this? Because once you start this and set things into motion there's no turning back. You understand that, don't you?"

"Just get out of here before I change my mind," he responded jokingly.

Cord walked back over to his bunk and retrieved his hat, placing it on his head before slipping on his vest. "Okay, so how does this work?"

"Hit me," Sage directed him as he offered up his jaw and braced it.

"Excuse me?" Cord asked, completely shocked by the request.

"You don't expect me to just let you waltz out of here

without me putting up some resistance. It needs to look like you got the better of me so I need you to hit me."

"Sage, I can't..."

"Your gun and gun belt are in my bottom desk drawer," Sage interrupted him to say as he braced for the blow. "Take my horse, for now, since yours is at the livery stables. You won't have time to get it out without wasting too much time and drawing unwanted attention to yourself. It's the quarter horse tied out front."

"I don't know what to say," Cord started. "I...I just don't have the words."

"I know, I know," Sage remarked solemnly. "Just be careful, Cord. You're a fugitive now. They'll be more than happy to hunt you down and kill you on the spot if they're provoked. Remember that while you're..."

Cord swung hard and fast, catching Sage off-guard and knocking him down flat onto the floor. It was a solid punch that Cord wanted to give him before Sage had time to brace for it so it would be more effective, and more convincing to those who would question its validity. Sheriff Connelly went down like a rock and did not move.

Cord took the cell door keys from Sage's hand and moved quickly to the outside door leading into the cells, closing and locking it behind him and dropping them just outside of the door so it would look like he had jumped Connelly and taken them from him. He retrieved his gun and gun belt from the drawer as Sage had advised him and quickly strapped it on, loosening the gun in its holster before walking over to the front door of the office. He gently pulled back the shade covering the window and peered outside for witnesses knowing there were bound to be someone who would see him. When only a minimal amount of people were visible, he casually opened the door and walked outside, closing it behind him as he walked over to Sheriff Connelly's horse and leisurely swung into the saddle, using the reins to turn the animal west, heading towards the edge of town at a simple gait.

West. Towards the only two towns in that direction for some distance: Calhoun and Benton Springs.

West. Towards this kid, Jesse Morse, the one person who could clear him, who would more than likely be heading to one of the two towns.

West. Towards Frank Quincey and his men.

West. Towards Madeline Stafford.

It took a few seconds for Sheriff Sage Connelly to regain his composure as to where he was when he was shaken awake by Deputy Tom Wills. It was after those first few seconds that he realized Wills was talking to him and becoming increasingly concerned that Connelly had yet to answer him back.

"Sheriff," he heard Deputy Wills call out again. "I said 'are you alright'?"

Sheriff Connelly nodded softly as he tried to gently shake the cobwebs from his brain and gather his thoughts. He was still sitting on the floor right outside of Cord's cell with Deputy Wills kneeling down beside him, his hand on the sheriff's shoulder trying to steady him enough to help him up when he felt coherent enough and ready to try it.

"What happened, sheriff?" Deputy Wills asked him as he was finally able to help the still-wobbly sheriff slowly to his feet.

"It was Cord," Sheriff Connelly stated as he cautiously made his way into the office and to his chair which he more or less fell into. He was still gathering his bearings as Wills continued pumping him with questions.

"Cord jumped you? Why would he do that?"

"Because I told him what Judge Hess said. I was standing

close to the cell talking to him and he reached over and grabbed me and pulled me close enough to grab the keys from my hand and knock me out."

Deputy looked at the sheriff through suspicious eyes. "He grabbed the keys from you and knocked you out?"

Sheriff Connelly looked up at Deputy Wills' face. He could tell by the man's expression that he was skeptical of the tale being woven for him. "That's the story," he reiterated with a blank look and a simple nod.

Deputy Wills nodded gently as the truth behind the tale struck home. "Oh, yeah, I'll bet that was quite a surprise."

"Yeah, it was," Sage conceded as he felt his tender jaw and moved it about trying to work out the tightness.

"Well, then," Wills added casually, "I guess we need to organize a posse, shouldn't we, sheriff?"

"There's no time for that," Sage responded in like manner. "We'll have to go after him ourselves."

"Okay," Wills responded. Sheriff Connelly and Deputy Wills grabbed their hats and Sage strapped on his gun belt as they exited the sheriff's office and out onto the boardwalk where Sage noticed that his horse was missing and suddenly remembered that he had instructed Cord to take it. Deputy Wills saw it, too. "You'll have to get a horse from the stables," Wills announced as he climbed into his saddle.

"There's no time for that, either," Connelly pointed out. He glanced around the streets and saw one of the towns-people on their horse walking towards them. Connelly ran over to meet him in the middle of the street. "Nelson! I need to borrow your horse. A prisoner just escaped and he stole mine."

The man called Nelson stared at Connelly as he pulled the horse to a stop. "Borrow my horse? But, sheriff, I'm headed home."

"I don't have time to argue with you, Nelson. Get down! I need your horse, right now!"

Nelson scoffed at the notion and reluctantly got down and was still holding the reins when Connelly snatched them from the man and swung into the saddle, kicking the beast into motion in one fluid move. Nelson was left standing in the middle of the street with his mouth hanging open as the shock at what had just occurred continued to wear away at him while other bystanders walked over to him to see what had just happened.

Sheriff Connelly and Deputy Wills rode towards the outskirts of town having brought the horses to a full gallop before they even reached the last building. There were only two possible places Cord could be heading, Calhoun and Benton Springs, with the nearest of the two being almost a full days ride, which Connelly had no intention of doing. They would pursue him for what seemed like an adequate amount of time before calling off the search and returning to Hurley, empty-handed and appearing defeated. The delay would give Cord the amount of time that he needed to put Hurley and his potential demise behind him, at least for the time being.

It was after sundown when Sheriff Connelly and Deputy Wills returned to Hurley, walking their horses into the quiet, virtually deserted streets and over to the sheriff's office. The two men climbed down, stretching their backs out once their feet had hit solid ground and trying to shake the dusty trail from their clothing. Connelly was the first to walk up to the door of his office and, as such, was the first to see the piece of paper protruding from the closed door. When he opened his door he removed the paper and read it:

Sheriff,
Come see me right away.

Judge Hess

"What's that?" Deputy Wills asked curiously. Sage read the note and passed it over to Wills, feeling it was without need of a comment. He removed his hat and hung it on the coat rack as he lazily walked past it, sinking into his chair with a relieving sigh, the ride having taken more out of him than he had expected. Wills picked up on the sheriff's lack of motivation. "Aren't you going over there?" Wills asked as he looked up from the note, a river of concern filtering through his words.

"Not right now," Sage responded as he closed his tired eyes and tried to rub the stiffness from his neck without much success. "He can wait."

"But isn't he going to be upset that you didn't?"

"Don't worry, he'll still be upset in the morning," Sage pointed out flatly as he leveled his look at the man. "He won't know what time we made it back to town. Besides, I'm too tired to get into it with him until I've had a good night's sleep. Considering what's just happened, it might be the last one I get for quite some time."

CHAPTER TEN

Sage Connelly's quarter horse instantly responded to Cord's tug on its bridle as it cantered into Benton Springs. Cord allowed the horse to continue its exhibition in front of the few townspeople who bothered taking the time to see the stranger who was coming into town.

The horse had been lively and spirited, showing Cord why the sheriff admired the animal so much. Although it wasn't his buckskin it was still a worthy substitution that he didn't mind, at least for the time being, but it still didn't replace the fact that he still longed for his beloved buckskin.

Cord pointed the horse to the first saloon he came to and climbed down, tying it off before walking inside. The atmosphere inside was quiet with only a few individuals scattered about who had collected there to quietly pass away the rest of the hot afternoon. Cord made his way over to the bar and waited for the chance to get the bartender's attention. He scanned the faces of those inside on the chance that the young man he was looking for would be among them, but he had no such luck. He hoped the bartender could help him since he didn't know how much time he had nor how many would be pursuing him. Right now, he was living on the edge of being surprised, and not in a good way, and if there was one thing that Cord Chantry did not like it was surprises.

The bartender finally took it upon himself to abandon his talk with one of the patrons and walked over to hear Cord's request. Cord could tell from the man's apathetic demeanor that he wasn't interested in going out of his way to offer any help.

"I need a whiskey and some information," Cord announced just loud enough for the man to hear him.

"That'll be two bits for the whiskey and the price of the information depends on what it is."

Cord fished out two coins from his vest pocket and tossed them onto the bar, glaring at the bartender with building impatience as he watched him finish pouring his drink. The bartender lazily sat the bottle down and braced his frame against the bar with outstretched arms as he waited for what Cord had to say.

"I'm looking for someone," Cord started. "Young kid, probably around twenty, brown hair, wearing a dark blue shirt, tan pants and a tan vest and wearing a black Hardee hat. Would have come by sometime around a few hours ago."

"Yeah, I seen him," the bartender said casually.

"Did he say where he was headed?"

"That depends on how much you're willing to pay," the bartender said casually with a coy smile. "How bad do you wanna find this fella?"

The snide comment was the final thing needed to set Cord off. *There could be a posse breathing down his neck even as he stood there playing games with this idiot. He didn't have time for this.* Without warning, Cord reached over the bar and grabbed the man by the front of his shirt and yanked him forward, slamming his stomach into the back of the bar with such force that it almost knocked the breath out of him as he leaned the top part of the man's body over the top of the bar towards him. The bartender could tell by the look in Cord's light, steely grey eyes that Cord was not in the mood for such nonsense and his attitude changed accordingly.

"Okay, okay, mister, I was just foolin'," the bartender spilled his knowledge. "Yeah, he was in here. Like you said, maybe a few hours ago."

Cord glared deep into the man's eyes as he continued. "Which way was he headed?"

"I don't know," he answered abruptly, but soon realized that it appeared Cord wasn't believing him as he continued to stare at him, his face set in grim, watchful lines. "That's all I know, mister, I swear."

Cord took the man's look as proof that he was telling him the truth and released his grip on him allowing him to straighten his shirt and gather himself, all the while never taking his eyes off of Cord. Cord reached into his pocket again and pulled out two more coins, bouncing them on the counter, their metallic sound being the only one that could be heard since the entire saloon had fallen deafly quiet from the commotion. He tossed back the shot and sat down the glass before walking to the door, his footsteps echoing across the wooden floor until he was outside standing in the sun.

He took in the streets on both sides, panning for unwanted interest directed at him. Without knowing what type of horse Jesse Morse was riding it was going to make it harder for him to clear out possible hiding places, assuming young Jesse was even still in town. It was possible he had only stopped off here for a quick drink and had decided to continue on through to Calhoun, a thought that Cord didn't want to have to consider. The further away from Hurley he got the farther he would have to escort Jesse Morse back so he could help Cord to clear his name. It sounded simple enough but there was a catch. He had no idea how willing the young man was going to be to have to return to Hurley, but it was safe to say it wasn't going to go over well with him. The last thing he wanted to have to do was to babysit a kid all the way back to Hurley while also trying to dodge a posse that he could assume was hellbent on killing him. *How had he gotten himself into such a mess?*

Bright and early the morning following Cord's escape, Sheriff Connelly walked over to Judge Hess' chambers to face his wrath. Connelly knew it wasn't going to be a pleasant encounter and had no idea where the meeting would lead him or what actions he would be forced to take now that Cord was considered to be an escaped murderer. Whatever it was, he already knew he wasn't going to like it.

Sheriff Connelly didn't have any reservations about what he had done to help Cord escape. He felt as if he had no other choice. Judge Hess was being far too harsh and he didn't appear to be taking Cord's life into consideration in all of this. It wasn't appropriate for a judge to automatically consider someone to be guilty without even having a trial. There was something else going on, that was for certain. Connelly hoped he would be able to find out exactly what it was that was spurring Judge Hess on before things got too far out of hand.

He had made it to the outer door of the clerk's office when he hesitated, his hand firmly gripping the door handle as he took in one last deep breath of nerve before opening it. He would have to face Judge Hess' clerk, Leonard Baker, first, a thought that was hard enough to take on its own and was almost as bad as dealing with Hess himself. Leonard would be gloating and condescending, there would be no doubt in his mind of that. He only hoped that he could refrain himself from lunging over the desk and strangling his tiny little neck with his bare hands. It would almost be worth the repercussions he would be forced to face just for the opportunity to do so.

Sage Connelly turned the handle and stepped into the room, catching Leonard's condescending look as soon as he made eye contact with him. Leonard followed up the pretentious stare with his usual smirk before he spoke.

"Judge Hess is furious with you," he stated before Sage could announce himself. He could tell by the remark that Leonard was enjoying himself immensely and was relishing in the turn of events, especially since he knew he would be able to hear everything through the door.

"Can you just tell him that I'm here," Sage snipped, cutting Leonard's gloating short while also trying to restrain the irritation in his voice.

"Oh, don't worry," Leonard responded with arrogant confidence before adding, "he's been expecting you, although you're about a day later getting here than you were supposed to be."

Sage didn't bother taking a seat as he knew Hess would be anxious to get started berating him. Leonard barely had enough time to announce Connelly's presence before he opened the door and ushered him inside, throwing him one last smirk before closing the door behind him. Judge Hess' expression said it all. This was not going to go well.

"What the hell happened, sheriff?!" Judge Hess started off as he flung his hands in the air for dramatic effect before Sage even had a chance to step into the room completely. "You had the man in custody and you let him go! What ineptitude! How in the world did you allow that to happen?"

Sage tried to stick to his lie. "I didn't let him go, your honor. I was talking to him and he jumped me and took the keys and escaped. He even took my horse."

Judge Hess' expression told Connelly that he wasn't

buying it. "How did you get close enough to him with the keys for him to take them away from you?"

"It just happened, your honor. I didn't plan it that way. I guess I didn't realize just how close I was to the cell door until it was too late."

"I understand you went after him," Jude Hess declared, changing the direction of the discussion. Connelly was still wondering how Hess would have found out about it in the first place, but he decided this wasn't the right time to ask him. "So, what happened? I take it from the fact that you didn't bring him back that he somehow got away."

"Yes, your honor. He knocked me out and by the time I came around he had been long gone for awhile."

Judge Hess was not happy with Sage's answers thus far. He shifted in his chair to try to dull his anger. "Which direction did he go? Can you at least tell me that? Do you even have an idea where he was going?"

Sage thought for a second before answering, not wanting to unwittingly give away more than he actually knew. "I heard that he was heading west."

"And you're telling me you never came across him?"

"No, sir. We tried tracking him for awhile, but he had such a head start on us that we were never able to pick up his trail."

"*We?* Who is '*we*'?"

"Deputy Wills and myself."

"That's it? You didn't even bring a posse with you?"

"No, sir. There wasn't enough time to get one together."

"That's completely unacceptable, sheriff. In fact, this whole situation is a huge disaster. Your incompetence has now allowed a killer to get away. What are we going to do about that? We can't allow him to just get away. He needs to be brought to justice."

"I agree, your honor."

Judge Hess paused his rantings for a second and glanced over at Sheriff Connelly. "I've never known or heard of you to fumble taking care of a prisoner before, sheriff. How is it that this particular man got the better of you?"

Sheriff Connelly tried to suppress his guilt. "I don't know, your honor. I guess these things just happen sometimes. It wasn't like I did it on purpose." Connelly knew he had over-stepped his innocence as soon as the words left his mouth. He tried to quickly cover them up with an additional comment. "Chantry was fast, your honor. He had obviously been looking for an edge."

"Well, you've put us in a fine mess now, sheriff, a fine mess indeed."

"I just need to get a posse together so I can go after him."

"No, you aren't," Judge Hess announced sternly. "I'm not putting the lives of these townspeople in jeopardy just to try to save your skin."

"Excuse me?" Connelly asked as the comment caught him by surprise.

"You've failed in your duties, sheriff. This wasn't just some drunk and disorderly you didn't lock up. This is a killer. We can't have these type of people allowed to roam freely and put other innocent people at risk trying to bring him in just because you aren't able to do your job."

"Don't worry, we'll get him."

"No, you won't," Judge Hess proclaimed. "You're fired."

The words cut Sheriff Connelly to his very core. He antic-ipated Judge Hess would be angry, possibly even furious for that matter, but to have him take his job away from him was not what he had been expecting.

"You're firing me?" Sage responded, even as the words came out of his mouth they didn't seem real.

"You left me with no choice, sheriff. Your incompetence lost a prisoner and possibly even put others in harm's way, or at least you'd better hope it didn't or else you'll be responsible for whatever happens. I'm putting your deputy in your job."

"But you don't have the authority to fire me," Sage insisted, realizing that he might as well speak up since confronting Judge Hess at this point wasn't going to cause him any more damage than he had already inflicted upon himself.

"Technically, you're right," Judge Hess admitted. "I don't actually have the authority to make such a change in town personnel, but believe me, I have the say in this town to get it done, regardless. All I have to do is call an emergency town council meeting and I can promise you that I have the pull in this town and I'll get the votes that I need to kick you out without any problem, especially when I tell them how much danger they're in by keeping you on. A town isn't going to jeopardize its safety for anyone, not even you. Now, are you going to step down quietly or do I have to embarrass you in front of the entire town even more than you have already done to yourself? Because if you force me to do that I can promise you that when I'm through with you you won't be able to get a job mucking out the stables."

Sheriff Connelly wanted to argue the point, but he knew that the judge was right. When he put it that way it was clear that he didn't have a voice in this, no matter how much he hated being bullied.

"Fine," Sage conceded with a disappointed look. "I'll step down."

"Smart move, sheriff," Judge Hess said while gloating. "I mean *Connelly*."

Hearing the statement hurt him almost as much as being fired.

Almost.

CHAPTER ELEVEN

Sage Connelly walked out of Judge Hess' chambers with his expression low and his spirits even lower. As he walked past Leonard Baker's desk he caught a glimpse of the man's sarcastic smirk radiating across his face, having obviously heard the entire exchange. The expression used up the last remaining morsels of Connelly's restraint. "Shut up, Leonard before I beat that smirk right off your face," he snapped at the man causing Leonard Baker's smile to abruptly disappear as Sage exited the outer door.

He hadn't seen this coming, although he wasn't necessarily surprised that Judge Hess had pulled that particular card to deal him. But, still, as he continued heading back to the sheriff's office he couldn't shake the notion that something wasn't quite right. This wasn't just about Hess dispensing law and order. There was something else going on. Judge Hess was in this for a different reason, just exactly what that was Sage wasn't sure, but it had something to do with making sure Cord was hanged, and quickly.

He stepped through the door of the office, feeling odd and out of place. The reality was finally setting in that this was no longer his office. Deputy Wills was waiting for him to return and quickly picked up on his uneasiness. "What's wrong, sheriff?"

Sage hung his hat and sat down. "Well, for one thing you don't need to call me that anymore."

"Why?" Deputy Wills asked and then just as quickly, the answer came to him. "He *fired* you?"

"Yep," Sage confirmed with a sharp nod as he added, "and he wants *you* to take it over."

Deputy Wills was shocked. "He wants to make *me* the *sheriff?*"

"Congratulations," Sage spoke as he removed the badge from his shirt and handed it to Wills, who reluctantly took it and stared at it as if he wasn't ready to pin it on.

"I can't do this, sheri… " Wills caught himself and paused out of embarrassment. "I don't know what to call you," Wills said as he faked a grin to break the awkwardness. "You've always been 'sheriff' to me."

"It'll take some getting used to, that's for sure," Sage reassured him.

"So what's next for you?"

Sage shrugged his shoulders and nodded. " I don't know about long-term, but right now I need to find Cord and warn him."

"Warn him about what?"

"Judge Hess is cooking something up and I'm not sure exactly what it is, but regardless of what it turns out to be what I do know is that Cord doesn't come out of this very well."

The last shreds of sunlight slid through the windows and across Judge Hess' desk as he finished making his notations in the top file on his desk. It had been a trying day with having to fire Sage Connelly and being concerned about Cord Chantry's whereabouts, but even as hopeless and out of sorts as things seemed to be it was still nothing that he couldn't handle, he was sure of that. All he needed was someone to come in and tie up the loose ends of this predicament for him and he knew just the person who could get it done.

An hour later, Judge Hess had dismissed Leonard Baker for the night so he could go over several cases in the quiet solitude of his office without the fear of being interrupted. Hess wanted to stay on top of the town's cases since it was vital for him to remain favorable in the eyes of the townspeople, something that he was having great difficulty accomplishing now due to Sage Connelly's blunders. Connelly had put him in a vulnerable spot and vulnerability was something that Hess would not tolerate, not if he was to successfully execute his plans.

Judge Rory Hess was a middle-aged man driven by an intense desire to succeed and an even more intense demand to make a name for himself. Originally from the east, he had seen the coming times of the evolving territory and wanted to get his foot in on the beginning of what he deemed to be an explosion of opportunity. He had been assigned to the territory just eight months earlier to replace his predecessor who had moved on, Hess believed, because he had outlived his usefulness. Hess had only briefly met the man and had determined right away that he was a weak excuse of someone who was sworn to dispense justice. Hess had not respected the man, believing him to be too soft and lenient on those who had willingly broken the law. Hess believed that such men should be punished and punished swiftly and harshly, but the man had not been willing to do what was necessary to keep order in the territory. His dismissal came at just the right time for Hess who was looking to advance his career, at whatever the cost to someone else. If it came at the demise of another's career, then so be it.

Hess' career was nothing short of pristine and distinguished, the only way he would accept it to be and his reputation for enforcing the law had followed him wherever he had presided. There was nothing and no one that was going to stand in his way and he intended to prove that at every opportunity he had.

Judge Hess had organized his papers on his desk for the following day to allow him to pick up where he had left off and had adjusted the lapels of his coat and was just about to remove his hat from the top of the coat rack when he heard the door open behind him. Hess sighed heavily as he resumed placing his hat on his balding head, despite the visitor having stepped into his office.

"Come back tomorrow," he barked in annoyance without even turning to face the person standing in his door. "I'm going home."

Judge Hess heard the door close and slowly turned towards it as he initiated another annoyed comment. "I said I'm..."

His comments and his thoughts were immediately stopped when he saw the man who had made his way into the office, his blunt, hardened features unscathed by the tone of Hess' voice or his words. The man's solemn expression did not break as he closed the door behind him and spoke. "You aren't going home just yet."

Despite the fact that he had summoned the man to his office, Judge Hess still retained a bit of reservation for having him there. Abel Prentiss was a cold man, the coldest of any individual he had ever encountered including any of the heartless and brutal men he had dealt with during his career as a prosecutor. He had seen some barbaric and inhumane actions committed by these men, things that would cause a man to lose his dinner just from their horrific description alone, but even they did not give him pause the way it felt to be in the same room with this man. Hess wanted to believe that a man could not be capable of the things he had heard Prentiss had done. Hess had heard these stories more than once, stories that he chose to believe for the sake of his own conscience, were embellished, stories that a man should never be capable of doing to another man. But he had a sneaking suspicion that the stories, however unnerving they sounded were, in fact, real.

"I thought I told you to wait until after dark to come here," Jude Hess scolded the man, weakly trying to maintain his tough composure as he decided to sit back down behind his desk.

Abel Prentiss spoke in his deep and booming baritone voice. "I didn't want to wait till dark. I came when I wanted. *You* sent for *me*, remember?"

Judge Hess turned his head slightly and stretched his neck off to the side as if his collar had suddenly become too tight for him. "Yes, I remember," Hess spouted as he hesitated before continuing. "I need you to take care of someone."

"Don't you always?" Prentiss recounted as he strolled over and took the chair opposite of Hess' desk, almost unable to fit into it. The man was massive, towering at almost six-feet four, his upper body thick and powerful. He carried his two-hundred-plus pounds well and with ease. Judge Hess eyed the man, finding it hard for him to believe that such a large man could move about as easily as he did which was evident from the fact that he had not even heard him come into the outer office.

"I need you to find a man who escaped from jail," Judge

Hess started. "Find him and bring him back here to stand trial."

"Trial for what? What did he do?"

"He killed a man."

"Is he dangerous?" Abel Prentiss asked nonchalantly.

Judge Hess was surprised by Prentiss' choice of words, knowing that he was asking based on the man's supposed reputation and not out of fear since there was no one that scared the man. "He could be considered that, yes. He's trouble."

Prentiss was unscathed by the comment. "If he's so much trouble, why bother keeping him alive?"

"Because I need for the people of this town to see me convict and sentence this man, that's why. It's important to my career."

Prentiss scoffed loudly. "Your career?" he uttered under his breath. "We both know you're so crooked they'll have to screw you into the ground when they bury you."

"Keep your voice down," Hess instructed in a harsh tone as his eyebrows furrowed. "I have a reputation in this town and I'll not stand by and watch you destroy that, do you understand?"

Abel Prentiss had been sitting back in his chair casually picking his teeth with a toothpick he had been savoring since before his arrival, his eyes focused on the folders sitting in front of Hess, but the comment caused him to cut his eyes up from under his hat brim at Judge Hess. It was clear he didn't appreciate the tone in Hess' voice and his icy stare confirmed just that. He slowly pulled the toothpick from his lips and hardened his stare. "You'd be well advised to watch how you speak to me. You understand me?"

Judge Hess swallowed hard, unsure of what to do knowing he had stepped over the line. It would not be beyond Abel Prentiss to pull his gun and kill him right there in his chair.

Prentiss cared so little about retribution that he would easily do so even if the room were filled with witnesses. Being alone with him would make it that much easier.

Suddenly finding himself in an uncomfortable situation, Hess decided he needed to try to repair the damage. "I'm sorry, its just that I need this to be taken care of as quickly and as clean as possible. It can't come back to me that I hired you. It needs to appear as if you acted alone."

"If you aren't hiring me then who's paying me?"

"I'll make it look like the territory is paying you. That way, it'll be all legal and legitimate, but you'll be reporting straight to me."

Abel Prentiss held the toothpick out in front of him and examined it for a few seconds, and then replaced it back in the same side of his mouth before responding. "How much?"

"I'm issuing a warrant for his arrest and offering a reward of three-thousand dollars."

"Five."

Judge Hess was annoyed by the figure. "*Five?* That's more than the typical reward in this type of situation. I think I'm being very generous even with offering three."

"You said he was dangerous *and* trouble. I need to be well paid for having to deal with 'dangerous' *and* 'trouble' and the price is five-thousand."

"But that's more than I was willing to offer."

"Then *you* go after him," Prentiss announced as he began to get up from the chair. Seeing Prentiss willing to leave so easily caused Hess to immediately respond.

"Wait, wait, wait," Hess jumped up from his own chair, waving his hand gently while doing so to try to stop the man from leaving. "Alright, five it is," he agreed with a sigh as he waited for Prentiss' response. His plea had worked and he was relieved to see the man sit back down as he continued to toy with his toothpick.

"So who is this man?" Prentiss asked.

"His name is Cord Chantry," Hess began. "He shot and killed a gambler in one of our saloons. Claims the gambler killed one of his friends in cold blood right in front of him."

"Why didn't you arrest him?"

"We did. Locked him up, too, but the sheriff allowed himself to get jumped and Chantry got away."

"Sounds like you need a new sheriff."

"I've already fired him and I put his deputy in his place."

"Why not have the deputy go after this Chantry fella? If you've already got a new sheriff then why do you need me?"

"Because he's not ready for that. Till now, he's only been a lowly deputy. This would be way over his head."

"Then why'd you put him as sheriff?"

Judge Hess was becoming increasingly annoyed by the series of questions, but tried to hide it. "I didn't have a choice. I needed someone in there immediately. But he's too complacent. I'm afraid this town is too much for him. I don't think he can handle it, but he'll have to do until I can think of something else."

"Then keep him out of my way," Prentiss warned. "I don't like having the law breathing down my neck and I ain't going to babysit."

"Understood."

"Why is it so important for you to get this guy?"

"Because I have political ambitions and I can't afford to let them get derailed."

"What kind of plans?"

Judge Hess leaned forward and placed his arms onto his desk. "A few years ago, Missouri became a state and was admitted to the union. It was just the latest step in how this territory is evolving. The frontier is disappearing, my friend, and with it goes the harsh, brutal living conditions, indian attacks, range wars over land and water and the other lawlessness that come when you don't have a controlled system in place. Becoming a state will change all of that. It will implement guidelines and statutes and the law will finally be much more easily enforceable."

"So Missouri became a state. How does that affect you?"

"Because I believe it won't be too far in the future before Wyoming is also made a state and admitted to the union and when that happens and it is recognized as a state, they're going to need a senator or maybe even two. When that day comes, I plan on being so well-known that I'll be the first one in line that they consider for the seat. That means that I need to have a clean record as territorial judge. Up till now, I did have that, but now this Chantry fella has ruined that for me unless I can get him and bring him back here to stand trial before the word gets out of his escape. I need to prove to the good people of this territory that I can maintain the peace while it's still a territory so they'll believe that I can maintain it when it becomes a state. That's where you come in."

Abel Prentiss' tone remained calm, unimpressed by Hess' ambitions. "I still say if you're just going to hang him anyway I don't see why you want me to go to all of the trouble of bringing him in alive."

"Because he needs to be made an example of to deter anyone else from coming into this town and killing someone," Judge Hess reiterated. "If you just kill him outright, no one will know that I had anything to do with him being brought to justice and convicted and I won't get the credit that I need. Thanks to me this is a sleepy, peaceful, law-abiding town. I intend on keeping it that way."

"When did he leave?"

"Yesterday afternoon."

"Direction?"

"He was heading west."

Prentiss stood and began slowly walking towards the door. "How do I get a description of him?"

"Go talk to Deputy, I mean Sheriff Wills," Judge Hess instructed him as he took out a piece of paper and a pencil. He scribbled something on the paper and folded it before handing it to Prentiss.

"What's this?" Abel Prentiss asked as he took the paper and glanced at it.

"That's a statement from me that the new sheriff is to cooperate with you in any way possible by divulging any information he has on Cord Chantry, including his description."

Prentiss started to leave but then stopped and turned to face the judge again. "Isn't he going to wonder who I am?"

Judge Hess shook his head gently. "Just tell him you're a bounty hunter and you heard about Chantry from me. That's all anyone needs to know."

CHAPTER TWELVE

The clerk at the hotel walked out from the back room in answer to the ringing bell on the counter. Besides the three saloons, this was the second hotel in Benton Springs that Cord Chantry had been to during his search for Jesse Morse. The clerk, an older small-framed man with a bushy mustache and a bad slicked-down combover, smiled as he came up to the counter where Cord was waiting. "Yessir, can I get you a room?"

Cord shook his head. "No, I'm just looking for someone."

The clerk flashed his practiced smile. "I'm sorry, sir, but I'm afraid our policy dictates that I can't disclose information on any of our customers."

"I know who I'm looking for, I just need to know if he's here."

"Is the purpose of this visit for business or personal?"

"Personal."

"Well sir, why don't you describe him to me and I'll tell you if you're in the right place."

Cord sighed, his patience growing tired of repeating the same thing to everyone he had encountered. "He's around twenty, blue shirt, tan pants and vest and wearing a black Hardee hat."

The description startled his memory. "Ah, yes, that gentleman *is* staying here," the clerk cheerfully acknowledged as he continued his persistent smile.

Cord's demeanor perked up from the news. "Which room is he in?"

The clerk looked back at his board to make sure he was correct before he answered. "Room seven. Up the stairs, second door on your right."

"Thanks," Cord responded with a simple nod as he turned and walked back outside to the surprise of the clerk. Since Cord didn't know how this was going to go down he decided to stack the odds more in his favor since there was a good chance that young Jesse Morse would not be willing to come peacefully. After climbing into his saddle, he walked the quarter horse around the hotel to the back entrance and dismounted, letting the reins drop.

He started up the stairs to the second floor. When he had reached the landing, he paused briefly to unhook the trigger guard and loosen the Colt in his holster, unsure of what he was about to encounter. He walked slowly down the short hallway picking up a small, wooden chair that was sitting on the hallway along the way and carried it with him to room seven and waited by the right side of the door, leaning his ear against it to detect any sounds he could hear coming from the room. Nothing. He rapped lightly on the door and waited. He could hear faint footsteps in the room, but no rustling or sudden steps. Then, he heard a man's voice.

"Who is it?" the man asked. Before Cord could respond he heard the sound of a gun being cocked. Cord drew his Colt while holding the chair with his left hand. He stepped back from the door and kicked it hard, busting the lock and flinging the door open. As soon as the door was wide enough,

Cord tossed the chair into the room just before he heard a gunshot fired from inside the room. He heard the bullet going into the floor where he had tossed the chair and he stepped in quickly, found his target and fired. The bullet struck the young man in his gun hand, causing him to drop his weapon as he clinched his now bleeding right hand with his left. Jesse Morse groaned through gritted teeth at the pain.

"What the hell did you do that for?!" Jesse Morse yelled as he clutched his hand up against his chest with blood seeping through his good hand and onto the top of his boots and the floor.

"I don't take kindly to being shot at," Cord stated as he holstered his gun. He walked over and pulled Morse's hand- kerchief from around his neck and began tying off the wounded hand. Jesse Morse initially tried to pull back away from him, but Cord grabbed his arm and held him in place as he looked him in the eye. "Hold still," Cord warned him. Initially, Morse resisted as he continued to try to pull back, obviously angered at being shot. Cord was losing his patience. "Be still or I'll shoot your other hand." Morse looked into Cord's eyes again and decided Cord was going to do it whether he wanted him to or not so he stopped resisting. Before Cord could finish tying off the wound, he heard foot- steps running up the stairs. He spun and drew his gun a few seconds before the clerk appeared in the doorway. When the clerk came into Cord's sight, he immediately halted his move- ments and stopped in his tracks. He looked to see Cord trying to bandage Morse's hand and the blood that had accu- mulated on the floor at his feet. All he could do was stare at Cord and Jesse Morse with his mouth hanging open.

"I'm going to get the sheriff!" the clerk announced as he turned and hurried down the hall and back down the stairs where he had come.

"Now you've done it, mister," Morse snapped out of anger as he jerked his newly-bandaged hand away from Cord. "They're going to lock you up for this!"

"Shut up," Cord answered calmly as he glanced down at the gun lying on the floor that Morse had just fired at him. It was River Holloway's pearl-handled Colt Paterson revolver. Cord reached down and picked it up. He looked it over before tucking it into his waistband.

"You trailed me and shot me for that gun?" Jesse Morse asked incredulously. "Are you crazy?"

"What, you're telling me you don't remember me?" Cord asked.

"Yeah, I remember you, alright," Morse said bluntly. "You killed that gambler in Hurley."

"I shot a man who was trying to shoot me," Cord corrected him. "If he had pointed a gun at you, you would've done the same thing."

"Maybe, but that still doesn't give you the right to shoot me over that stupid gun."

"Well, you should have thought about that before you stole it."

"It's just a gun. It's not worth that much," Morse argued, trying to make his case.

"It was evidence in a shooting, a shooting that now looks like I committed murder since you took the other man's weapon. I've got the law after me because of your interference."

"That's still no reason to shoot me!" Jesse Morse spouted.

"And what were you planning on doing to me just now?" Cord asked as he looked at Morse with disinterest. "C'mon. Let's go."

"What? Where are we going?"

"The doctor's office is right next door. I'm going to take

you there and get that hand looked at and then we're going to Hurley so we can clear this up."

"I'm not going to Hurley!"

"Oh, yes you are," Cord demanded. "And you're gonna tell the sheriff there exactly what happened. *Exactly*."

"I'm telling you, mister, that I'm not going to Hurley!"

Cord grabbed Morse by the arm and turned him to look into his eyes while Morse tried to pull back. "You'll either get on your horse and ride willingly or I'll hog tie you across your saddle and lead your horse there myself. It doesn't matter to me how you get there, but one way or another you're going to Hurley."

Jesse Morse looked into Cord's light grey eyes and felt a wave of nerves come over him. It was the first time he realized that this man wasn't going to take 'no' for an answer. Morse believed every word Cord was telling him and decided it was in his best interest not to push this man too far. He loosened his stance and allowed Cord to lead him out the door. As they walked over to the landing of the stairs they heard a voice call out.

"Stop where you are!" A man shouted. Cord looked down to see a man with a badge standing at the bottom of the stairs, his gun drawn and pointed at him. Cord froze in his tracks while still holding Jesse Morse's arm tightly.

"Take it easy, sheriff," Cord started to explain. "I'm just taking this man back to Hurley. He's a witness in a shooting."

"You a lawman?" Sheriff Nix asked as his unwavering gun remained focused on Cord.

"No, I was in a shooting there that was self-defense and this man was a witness to it."

"He's lying, sheriff!" Morse yelled, his face filled with fear. "He's trying to kill me! Look at what he did!" Morse shouted as he held up his wounded hand for the sheriff to get a good look at. "He's already shot me! Help me, sheriff!"

Sheriff Nix pushed his gun more towards Cord. "Let him go!" he demanded.

"Sheriff, I need him to go…"

"You don't need nothing!" Sheriff Nix stated firmly. "It's obvious he doesn't want to go with you and since you've already shot him I have to be concerned about his safety. I've already got you for assault. You let him go until I can sort this thing out. Do it now!"

Jesse Morse was trying to pull away from Cord's grip, but Cord refused to release him. He was trying to think of the best way out of this with the least amount of trouble, but Sheriff Nix wasn't going to give him that kind of time. "I said let him go!"

Cord considered his chances of drawing on the sheriff. It was obvious that the man looked uncomfortable holding a gun, probably because he didn't have to use one very often. He had heard of the sheriff before, about how much of a coward he was and how he had allowed Frank Quincey to run over him and his position. The entire town knew Nix was afraid of Quincey, but they allowed Nix to retain his job as sheriff because the truth of the matter was, the townspeople were afraid of Frank Quincey even more.

"I'm not going to tell you again, mister, drop that gun!" Nix ordered.

Cord tried once more to appeal to the sheriff. "I need to get him back to Hurley to settle a shooting," he stated firmly, his eyes hardened from the standoff.

Sheriff Nix stood his ground. "If he's so important then I'll telegram the law there and get their side of the story."

The offer didn't sit well with Cord. If Sheriff Nix wired Sage Connelly he would be forced to tell Nix that he, Cord, was an escaped fugitive. That would not only ruin his credibility but it would also bring Sheriff Nix down on Cord, not to mention ruin any chance Cord had of bringing Jesse Morse back to clear his name. No matter how Cord looked at it, the whole situation was quickly going south.

Before Cord could give his answer, two more men ran up and stopped beside Sheriff Nix, both with their guns drawn and pointed in his direction. Cord noticed that one of the men was wearing a deputy's badge. Cord knew that this was only going to strengthen Sheriff Nix's demands that much more. He decided it wasn't worth the risk of a shootout and he released Jesse Morse's arm. Morse pulled his arm away as soon as he felt Cord's grip loosen and cast a disgusted look at him before he started towards the stairs. Sheriff Nix's face showed satisfaction at the small victory, which only worked to empower him even more. "Now, throw down your gun, right now."

Cord quickly weighed his options. If he gave up his gun he would be arrested and put in jail until the authorities from Hurley came to get him and there would be no getting out again, the judge there, the same judge that wanted him dead, would most assuredly see to that. Cord knew he had no choice.

As Jesse Morse was about to reach the top of the stairs Cord kicked his foot out and booted Jesse forward. The push sent Morse flying off the landing and tumbling down the stairs. It was just the distraction that Cord needed. As Sheriff Nix and the two men were distracted by Morse coming down the stairs towards them, Cord turned and ran down the hallway but not before the men got off two shots which landed in the walls of the hallway right next to where Cord was passing. He hurried down the back stairs and jumped onto his horse, kicking it into motion as he heard the second floor door flying open and a barrage of gunshots pelting the ground around him as he rode swiftly away.

So much for his plan to clear himself.

CHAPTER THIRTEEN

Madeline Stafford was hanging up the last of her wet clothes on the clothesline when she saw the trail of dust being kicked up by an approaching rider. She paused, waiting for the man to come closer so she could determine if she needed to go back inside or if it were safe for her to wait there out in the open. When he was close enough she felt a sense of relief and jubilation at the sight of Cord Chantry.

Encouraged by Cord's enticing, the quarter horse galloped the remaining hundred yards up to Madeline stopping at the hitching rail as she walked the short distance over to him. After climbing down and tying off the horse they hugged and followed it up with a brief kiss. "Well, this is a pleasant surprise," Madeline said as she hugged him again and then separated and looked into his eyes. "I thought you were still on a cattle drive."

"I was," Cord started, not really sure how much of the story he wanted to share with her. "Then I decided to go see Sage, Tom and Nathan in Hurley."

"Oh, good," she mused with a cracked smile. "I didn't know you were going over there. So, how are they?"

"Sage and Tom are fine. I didn't have time to see Nathan. I'll see him on my next trip. How are you doing?"

"We're fine here," Madeline answered while wiping her forehead with the tail of her apron. "Bree's husband, Kyle, is out with one of their neighbors bringing in a herd of cattle. The neighbor said if Kyle helped him, he would give he and Bree ten head of cattle as payment to start their own herd. He should be home sometime tomorrow."

Cord hesitated, trying to fain interest in the story while also trying to hide his discomfort in withholding his own story as it had unfolded. The pause was enough to alert Madeline, her cheery smile quickly falling away as she picked up on his hesitation.

"Cord? What's wrong? What happened?" she asked inquisitively.

He waited, unsure of just how to break the news to her because once he started, there would be questions, questions that he would have to answer. Madeline was not the type of woman to let things go by the wayside. She would want to know every last detail and she wouldn't stop until she had them.

"*Cord?*" She asked again, this time with more concern in her voice.

He decided it was best to just tell her and get it over with. "I ran into River Holloway."

The mention of the man's name caused Madeline to gasp as her eyes focused even more intently on Cord's words. "River? Where did you see him? Did he see you?"

"Maddie, I killed him."

This time the gasp was even more pronounced as she covered her mouth with her hand. It was several seconds before she was able to resume talking. "How...how did this... what happened?"

Cord took in a much-needed deep breath before he

began. "When I got to Hurley, I went straight to see Sage and Tom Wills. We were talking and I told them I was going to be in town for awhile to see them and Nathan. Sage told me that River had come into town a week or so earlier and that he thought he might still be around."

"Why would he tell you that? He knows how you feel about him. Why not just let it go?"

"He was afraid if I didn't know to be on the lookout for him that I would accidentally run into him. He wanted me to be prepared for seeing him."

"Where did you find him?"

"In the saloon. He was playing cards with some other fellas. I walked up to him and told him I was bringing him in to Sage's office."

"Why wouldn't Sage just go arrest him himself?"

"Because he didn't have jurisdiction where Billy Richmond was killed. He wanted me to wait for the federal marshall to come so he could arrest him and we would be witnesses at the hearing."

"Sounds like a good plan. Why didn't you do that?"

Cord could see he was losing her being on his side. "It had been a long time since we saw him last. I was afraid River would leave town and I'd miss my opportunity to bring him in."

"But it wasn't *your* job to bring him in, Cord," Madeline chided, her stance becoming noticeably more rigid. "So instead of trying to solicit the help of the law you just shot him?"

"I told him to get up and go with me. He refused and then he pulled a gun. *This* gun," Cord said as he tapped the butt of the pearl-handled Colt Paterson in his waistband.

"So it was self-defense, right?"

"It was, but there was a young kid there and he and another guy walked over to check on River to see if he was dead. Somewhere in the commotion, the kid took River's gun and left without me seeing him. I had to track him down here to Benton Springs."

"Is *he* dead, too?"

"No, I caught up with him and tried to bring him back to Sage to verify that it was self-defense, but he got away."

Madeline looked puzzled and worried by the statement. "What does that mean, 'he got away'?"

"I got him out of his hotel room and I was bringing him down to the horses when the sheriff and a couple of others came in and stopped me."

"And this kid got away?"

"The sheriff took him from me. Thought I was kidnapping him or something. I had to leave town in a hurry because they were going to arrest me."

"But you said the gunfight was self-defense."

"It was, but it was dark in the saloon and this kid was the only one who saw River's gun. He grabbed it before anyone else made it over to the table. Everyone else thinks I shot River when he was unarmed because he didn't get off a shot."

"What did Sage say about this?"

"He had to arrest me, but then he let me out. Made it look like a jail break."

Madeline shook her head as she tried to gather the facts that Cord had given her. "So you shot River, got arrested and then Sage faked your escape?"

Cord nodded, although he knew the whole setup sounded too bizarre to be true. "Yeah."

Madeline nervously ran her hands through her hair as she took a few steps back, her eyes widened, her mind trying to process everything that she had just heard. "Oh, my gosh, Cord. You're a fugitive. You're a wanted man."

Cord tried to reach over to touch her to comfort her. "Maddie..."

"Don't 'Maddie' me," she snapped at him as she retreated from his grasp. "What are we going to do now? Tell me, Cord. What do we do now that you're wanted for murder?"

"I'll think of something," Cord tried to assure her, but she wasn't listening.

"'What? What are you going to think of? You can't be around here, not around my brother and my sister-in-law and the baby...*the baby*. Cord, they have a new baby. You can't bring all of this drama around them. It's going to get dangerous, a lot more dangerous, you know it is. This is only the beginning. It isn't fair to them. Someone could get hurt or even killed."

"Believe me, I'm not going to let that happen," he said in an attempt to convince her. "I'll get all of this cleared up, I promise. I'll make sure it doesn't affect you or your brother and his family."

"How are you going to do that, Cord? You're a fugitive. You don't even have anyone who can help you, certainly not Sage." She paused as she realized the implication. "And what about Sage? How is this going to affect him? He's sworn an oath to arrest you if he sees you so you can't even ask him for help."

"I'll think of something," Cord repeated, hoping that by hearing it again she would somehow believe him this time.

A thought suddenly occurred to Madeline. "What if someone else comes after you?"

Cord looked at her curiously. "What do you mean?"

"If you're wanted won't you have a reward on your head? Isn't there a risk of someone else coming after you to claim it?"

"You mean like a bounty hunter?"

"Yes."

"No. Word wouldn't have gotten out that quickly. Don't

worry. It hasn't been long enough for a bounty hunter to get involved."

Sheriff Tom Wills was filing papers when the door to his office opened. He turned to see the largest man he had seen in quite some time, if ever. The man stopped in the doorway as if waiting for Sheriff Wills to acknowledge his presence which he did. "Can I help you?"

Abel Prentiss stepped into the office closing the door behind him and turned back towards Wills. "You the sheriff?" Prentiss asked flatly. Sheriff Wills was not only surprised by the man's size, but by the deepness of his voice which seemed to match perfectly with his stature.

"I'm Sheriff Wills," he acknowledged as he wondered where this was going. "What can I do for you?"

Abel Prentiss walked the few steps over to Wills as he pulled a folded piece of paper from his shirt pocket as he maneuvered a toothpick. "Judge Hess told me to give you this."

Sheriff Wills looked the paper over and looked back at Prentiss with renewed concern. "You a bounty hunter?"

"That's right, and I need some information on Cord Chantry. I heard he escaped and that he's wanted for murder."

Wills glanced back down at the paper and then back at Prentiss, a look of wonder glossing over his face. "You found out about that awful fast," the sheriff indicated. "How did you hear about it?"

Prentiss reached over and removed the paper from the sheriff's hand and replaced it in his pocket as he spoke. "Does it matter? The fact is, I'm here now and I need information on this man. Judge Hess assured me that you would be willing to cooperate. Since this man is now a fugitive from the law and I'm sworn as a agent of the law I have a legal right to do that, don't I, sheriff?"

"Yeah, you do. I was just curious how you found out about him that fast, that's all. Did Judge Hess hire you?"

Abel Prentiss ignored the comment and stood silent, waiting without saying anything as if he didn't feel it necessary to talk about it any further. It was clear to Wills that that part of the conversation was over. After a few tense seconds, Sheriff Wills walked back to his desk and pulled out a piece of paper and a pencil and began writing, but just as he started Prentiss spoke up.

"What are you doing?"

Wills was surprised that he had to ask. "I'm writing you a description."

"Just tell me. I don't need it written down."

Sheriff Wills stopped writing and studied Prentiss. "Well, he's in his late twenties, a few inches shorter than you, medium build, black hair, wears a black Stetson. His most telling feature that makes him easy to spot are his eyes, they're a light grey. He normally rides a buckskin, but when he escaped he stole Sheriff Connelly's quarter horse so I don't know which one he'll be on when you catch up with him."

"Where was he headed?"

"He went west. I don't know if he was headed to Calhoun or Benton Springs. Those are the only two towns anywhere close in that direction," Wills watched the man standing and quietly staring a him as if he were insignificant. The look the man gave him was unsettling. "I...didn't know if you knew that."

"Is that all?"

Wills searched for any information he might have overlooked so there would be less likely of a chance of a return visit. He didn't want this man in his office again, if at all possible. "No, I think that's it."

"Thanks," Abel Prentiss said as he turned for the door, but Sheriff Wills stopped him with a question.

"Just out of curiosity, how much is the bounty on Chantry?"

Prentiss looked back at Wills as he removed his toothpick. "Five thousand." He paused a second before adding. "Preferably alive," as if he had guessed what Wills' next question would be. "Anything else?" he asked.

"No, that's all."

Abel Prentiss replaced the toothpick and opened the door, closing it behind him as he left without uttering another word. Sheriff Tom Wills was glad to see the man leaving. He walked over to the window and gently pulled back the shade so he could make sure that Prentiss was, in fact, heading out of town. The large man stepped into the saddle of his massive tan-colored dun, a fitting ride considering the size of the man riding it. As Abel Prentiss tugged on the reins, he glanced over at the window catching Sheriff Wills stealing a glance at him, as if he had expected to see the lawman watching him. The last thing Sheriff Tom Wills saw was the sly grin spread over Prentiss' face as he headed west after Cord Chantry.

CHAPTER FOURTEEN

An afternoon breeze licked at Sage Connelly's face as he took a perfectly-timed break from chopping firewood. Siting in the blazing sun, he felt the trail of sweat running down the crevasse of his back and down to the waistband of his pants. His breathing was starting to level out from the exertion, but it felt good to be out doing physical work again after being forced to stifle his movements for so many months until just recently when he had properly healed, or at least what could be considered as such.

His side had begun to ache from the strenuous movements, a lingering effect from being shot there less than a year earlier by one of Frank Quincy's men. Although the outer wound had healed properly as well as could be expected according to Doc Ballen's standards, the residual internal damage was for good and something he had reluctantly been forced to accept, along with the limitations that came with it.

Sage sat down on the chopping block and wiped his forehead with his bare arm while he gathered his breath. This time of day would typically find him making his mid-day rounds through the streets of Hurley, but he had been forced to accept the fact that those days were now behind him. It felt weird not to be strolling through town conversing with all of the townspeople, checking on the incoming stages, visiting with the various business owners and mingling with his friends. It was also strange not to have a badge pinned to his chest. It was the first time in many years that he hadn't worn one and he wondered just how long it would be before he accepted that he would never have one pinned on him again, a least not if Judge Hess had anything to say about it.

Being a sheriff had meant everything to him. It had made him who he was and had shaped his life into allowing him to feel as if he was making a difference. Having never married, Sage Connelly had devoted the best years of his adult life to keeping the peace and order in Hurley and for that the people of the town respected him and his job. Knowing that he could always be relied on made the town a much better place. To that, they were grateful. But he had already accepted the fact that they would soon forget him as long as someone else was there to fill his shoes.

He had the utmost respect for Tom Wills, he always had, but despite that there was still that lingering, nagging thought in the back of Sage's mind that made him wonder if Wills was up for the challenges that came with the job of being sheriff. He had no ill feelings for Tom Wills about taking over his job for he knew it wasn't Wills' idea and wished him all of the success that he could hope for his friend, but he still worried about him, nonetheless. Wills had never been forced to stand up to an angry crowd or to step in and break up a tense moment between two gunmen looking to settle a score. He wondered if his friend had the nerves that would be needed to do so. He hoped his apprehension was unwarranted.

Sage was about to force himself to get up and get back to work when he heard the distinct sound of an approaching horse. Judging by the galloping movement the animal was making the rider was in somewhat of a hurry to reach him. Sage remained seated on his stump until he saw Tom Wills coming down the road towards him. Once he was close enough, Sage could tell by the expression on Tom's face that this was not going to be a pleasurable visit. Wills stopped his horse short of Sage and quickly climbed down. The first thing that Sage thought was that it hadn't taken Wills long for things to get out of hand.

"Sheriff, what brings you out here?" Sage asked jokingly trying to break the tense mood while suddenly feeling the awkwardness of addressing someone else with that title.

"Sage, do you know where Cord is?"

Sage looked at Tom Will's face and saw that his expression was clearly one of worry so he abandoned his attempt at humor. "No, I haven't heard from him since he left, escaped. Why?"

Tom walked closer to Sage. "A man came in looking for information on Cord. A bounty hunter."

"A bounty hunter? This soon?"

Tom Wills nodded.

"Did you know who he was?"

"No. I've never seen him before."

"What did he look like?"

"Very stern. Very menacing. Big guy."

"Well, Cord is a big man."

"Not this big. Sage, this fella was huge."

The description was interesting. At six-foot-two, he had always considered Cord to be a large man, but for Tom Wills to imply that this stranger was even larger when compared to Cord would be something to see.

"Did he give you his name?"

"Judge Hess put it on the paper. Abel Prentiss is his name.

Judge Hess gave him a note instructing me to cooperate in helping him find Cord."

"*What?*"

"Yeah," Wills continued. "I read it myself. Judge Hess said to give him a full description and any information I had about his whereabouts."

"Did you?"

"I didn't want to. I felt bad about it, but I felt like I had to."

Sage nodded. "You did the right thing. Believe me, the last thing you want is to cross Judge Hess or we'll both be out of a job."

"What am I going to do, Sage? I feel like I betrayed Cord."

"It's not your fault, Tom. Judge Hess has got it in for Cord and he means to get him one way or another. Apparently now he's brought in this bounty hunter to do his dirty work for him."

Tom paused briefly before he asked something he had wanted closure on. "Sage, you let Cord go free, didn't you?"

"No, he escaped."

"Sage?"

"It's better this way. The less you know the better it'll be for you."

"Sage, it's me. You can tell me the ruth. At this point, it isn't going to matter."

Sage looked up at Tom, suddenly feeling the pressure of admitting to him what he had done. "I couldn't let him hang, Tom, not without him getting a fair trial and we both know Judge Hess wasn't going to allow that to happen. If I had left Cord in that jail cell he was as good as dead before the investigation ever even started. I didn't want that on my conscience."

"I understand, Sage, really I do, but it ended up costing you your job."

"Better my job than Cord's life."

"Sage, what do I do about Cord? If this bounty hunter catches up with him he'll bring Cord in and your little gesture of humanity won't have mattered because he'll still end up dead. Judge Hess will see to that. He has to be warned."

Tom Wills was surprised when he saw Sage stand and reach for his shirt. "What are you doing?" he asked even though he knew Sage Connelly well enough to already know the answer.

"I'm going to find Cord and warn him to get out of the territory."

"Sage, are you sure you want to get involved in this mess anymore than you already are? It's only a matter of time before Judge Hess finds out that you intentionally helped Cord escape and then he'll be sure to come after you, too. You'll be ruined from ever working anywhere around here again, especially as a lawman."

"It doesn't matter, Tom. It's too late for that anyway. Judge Hess has to be stopped. If he can do this to Cord so easily then he can do it to anybody. He has the power and the pull to conveniently break the law and still get away with it. Although I don't condone Cord killing River I still under-stand why he did it. And it was self-defense. If it had been you or I we would have done the exact same thing, you know that. Even if it wasn't the law says a man is entitled to a fair trial before being found guilty. You know Judge Hess isn't going to do that, he's already admitted it. If I let them bring Cord in then I'm no better than they are because I'll be condemning an innocent man and I might as well throw away everything I've ever stood for as a lawman."

"Sage, you know I can't..."

Sage held up his hand to stop him, already aware of what

Tom was going to say next. "It's alright," he assured Tom. "I understand. I don't expect you to get any more involved in this. This is my decision. I'm the one who's choosing to go warn Cord. This town needs you, Tom, especially with someone like Hess in charge. The people of Hurley need someone who'll stand up to him when it's needed and from now on that's going to have to be you." Sage finished putting his shirt on and grabbed his hat from on top of a nearby log, placing it on his head.

Tom followed Sage over to the barn where he started saddling Cord's buckskin that he had recovered from the livery stables since Cord had relieved him of his own horse when he had fled. Tom felt as if he should say something, but he was at a loss for words as to exactly what that was. He knew Sage Connelly well enough to know that he wasn't going to change his mind. Tom started to feel guilty. He felt as if he had brought the trouble and dropped it off on Sage's front porch for him to deal with. Now, Sage was going to get involved with a bounty hunter whom they knew very little about and who was unpredictable, which made him dangerous in the worst kind of way.

"How are you going to find Cord?" Tom finally asked as Sage cinched the last of the saddle belts underneath the horse.

Sage continued working on the belts as he answered. "Well, first I'm going to try the only two places I know he would probably be going. First, I'll try Maddie's place and then if that doesn't pan out I'll go to the Walking A ranch where Cord works. He's on the run so he's sure to be at one of those two. If not, at least somebody will be able to tell me where he's headed." Sage finished with the saddle and pulled Cord's Winchester from its scabbard to check it for ammo. Tom stood quietly wishing there was another way.

"Sage, is there anything I can do to help you?"

"Well, you can finish chopping my firewood," Sage answered with a faint grin as he replaced the rifle in the scabbard.

"No, I'm serious, Sage. Tell me if there's any way I can help."

Sage looked at his friend. *He had always been that*, he thought. *Always been a good friend*. "No, Tom, I don't think so. You need to stay out of this as much as possible. I know you want to help, but it's for your own good."

"Listen to me, Sage because I'm warning you. This bounty hunter, Prentiss, I've got a bad feeling about him. When I looked into his eyes it's as if he were dead inside, like he had nothing to lose and nothing to care about. I've never come across anyone that felt so inhuman. It's like he's not a person, but more like a wild animal that's been put into motion and won't stop until he's done what he was told to do. I'm telling you this, Sage, because you have to be careful. This guy is dangerous, I mean *really* dangerous. As soon as you meet him you can tell that he's capable of doing anything that needs to be done. If Judge Hess specifically hired him then you know he has to be pretty bad."

"It's alright, Tom, I'm just going to find Cord and tell him to get out of the territory, go somewhere that they don't know him and start over."

"You know he isn't going to do that," Tom argued. "He isn't about to leave Maddie behind and he sure isn't going to risk taking her with him and possibly seeing her get hurt from getting caught up in all of this, especially with bounty hunters after him. He's got the odds stacked up against him. What choice does that leave him? To stand and fight?"

"That's all he has," Sage noted. "And if I know Cord Chantry, that's exactly what he'll do."

CHAPTER FIFTEEN

With her hand leveled over her eyes to shield away the bright
sunshine, Madeleine Stafford watched from her brother's
front porch as Cord Chantry rode off towards the Walking A
ranch. She had not liked the way they had left things. It had
been their first fight, or at least what she chose to call a mild
disagreement, since they had started seeing one another.
Cord had been stubborn and distant from the beginning
when she had met him on that fateful stage ride, but over
time he had learned that she was different. He had lowered
his guard with her, allowed her to step into his world and his
thoughts, made her feel as if he trusted her, which was no
small achievement. But now? Now, she didn't know what to
think. She knew this was bad, but just how bad she wasn't
really sure which made her wonder that much more. *Was he
telling her the full truth?*

   She watched until he was out of sight before she walked
back over and went back to hanging the remainder of her
clothes with their discussion going through her mind. When
she had finished, she went inside and began cooking supper.
There was idle chit-chat between her and her sister-in-law,

but her mind was elsewhere. All she could think about was Cord, the situation he had gotten himself into and, most importantly, how he was going to get out of it or if that were even a possibility. She didn't like the odds and from what she could tell there didn't seem to be any way that they were going to get any better.

The sun had set and the evening was upon them as Maddie cleaned up the dishes and helping clean up as her sister-in-law started getting the baby ready for bed. With her brother gone out of town she was handling the household chores while her sister-in-law focused solely on taking care of the baby. Exhausted and still unable to get Cord and his predicament out of her mind, she stepped outside to retrieve more wood to keep the fire going through the crisp night that was ahead of them.

She was stacking small pieces of wood onto the crook in her arm when she heard what she thought was a rider approaching. She strained her eyes to look off into the distance, but it was impossible to see very far out, much less a great enough distance to identify an incoming rider. She immediately dropped the firewood onto the ground and hurried back into the house.

Once inside, she closed the door and placed the wooden bar across the back of it for extra measures. She walked over to the lantern nearest to her and blew out the flame before grabbing her brother's handgun from off the table, a safety measure he had insisted on before he had left to go on his trip. Right about now, she was grateful for his concern. The sudden darkness in the front room caused her sister-in-law, Bree, to call out from her bedroom where the only lantern was still burning "Maddie? What's going on?"

"Just stay where you are," Maddie warned her. "Someone's coming."

"Who is it?" Bree asked innocently, but with a hint of fear.

"I don't know," Maddie responded as she continued to peer out the front window. She turned and was annoyed to see that Bree had stepped out of the bedroom and into the front room in he open as she gently rocked her baby to try to get it to sleep.

"I told you to stay in the bedroom," Maddie berated her as she left her post and quickly ushered Bree and the baby back into the bedroom. "Now stay in here until I tell you it's safe to come out, alright?"

"Maddie, you're scaring me," Bree admitted as she clutched her baby tighter, the concern very evident on her face.

Maddie could see how anxious the situation was making Bree. What they didn't need right now was for Bree to fall apart giving Maddie something else to have to worry about. She had to calm her down before she became hysterical. "It's gonna be alright," Maddie tried to bring her anxiety down by calming the tone of her voice. She took in a deep breath and continued in a more relaxed tone. "Bree, I just need you to stay with the baby, okay? I'll handle this."

Bree flashed her a forced smile and nodded as she stepped back into the bedroom so Maddie could close the door behind her. She walked back over to the front window, picking the handgun back up along the way. When she settled back in by the window she glared outside. All she could make out was the silhouette of a man on a horse, nothing else. The rider was coming at a casual walk, but still coming. She doubted it would be anyone wishing to harm them, she kept telling herself, or else they wouldn't be so brazen with their approach to the home, especially not knowing who all was inside and if they were armed. She watched in silence as they stopped at the hitching rail and climbed down, taking the time to tie off their horse. It was only when the rider was stepping up onto the front porch that Maddie cocked her gun and waited off to the side of the window with her back pressed against the wall.

A knock at the door startled her, despite her knowing it was coming. She held the gun in front of her and remained quiet, choosing to make whomever was at the door to speak first.

"*Maddie?*"

At first, Maddie thought she recognized the voice, but she wasn't exactly sure. "*Sage?*"

"Yeah, it's me. Open up. I need to talk to you."

Maddie's relief flooded over her as she uncocked the revolver and laid it on the table before she removed the wooden bar and opened the door, a smile of relief flashing over her face when she saw Sage's face. Sage looked just as relieved.

"Oh, Sage, I'm so glad you're here," Maddie gushed while placing her hand on Sage's arm, as if she were making sure he was real. "Come in, come in," she said anxiously, ushering him in and closing the door behind her. He waited just inside the door as she replaced the wooden bar and led him over to the kitchen so she could light a lantern. As the glow increased in intensity, she turned to her friend. "What brings you out here?"

Just then, the bedroom door opened and Bree stepped out to check on who had arrived and was both surprised and relieved to see Sage there. "Oh, hi, Sage," she said cheerfully.

"Hi, Bree," Sage responded with a simple wave. She started to speak, but then she caught a glimpse of Maddie's troubled expression and realized that her discussion with Sage was a serious one so she stepped back into the room and closed the door. Sage waited until he was sure it was closed before he continued in a quieter voice.

"Maddie, Cord is in trouble," Sage blurted with more fervor than he had intended.

"Yes, I know," Madeline responded, feeling somewhat relieved that what he was telling her was nothing new. "He came by earlier today and told me about what happened with River and everything." Sage appeared to be confused by the remark. Madeline picked up on his expression turning curious. "What? What's wrong?"

"He told you everything? How could he? Maddie, how could he have already told you about the bounty hunter? He didn't even know."

Maddie's face went flush as the words sank in. All she could think of was Cord assuring her that there was no one coming after him, but she knew he wouldn't intentionally lie to her even if it was to protect her. That could only mean that he really didn't know about it.

"Did you hear me, Maddie?" Sage repeated while grabbing her hand to draw her attention. "I said Cord has a bounty hunter looking for him."

"Yes...yes, I heard you, Sage," Maddie spoke softly as she stared off into nothing, the seriousness of the situation beginning to sink in. She had feared this, although she had never mentioned that fear to Cord when he told her about shooting River, she had feared it, just the same. Now, it had come to fruition, as if she had willed it to be. She stared off into the room, initially unable to speak but finally gathering herself enough to respond. "Who is he?" she asked, knowing she would not recognize the name, but still needing to know, regardless for her own sake.

"Abel Prentiss," Sage told her. "He was hired by the territory's judge, Judge Hess, the same man who fired me."

"You were *fired?*" Maddie exclaimed.

"Yeah," Sage reluctantly admitted.

"Why? Why would they fire you?"

"Not 'they', *him*. Judge Hess," Sage reiterated. "He fired me because I helped Cord escape."

"Oh, no," Maddie said, feeling Sage's disappointment. "What are you going to do?"

"Right now I'm going to find Cord and warn him."

Maddie glanced over at Sage. He could see the fear in her eyes. Fear for the situation and fear for Cord. "This bounty hunter, is he dangerous?"

"Yeah, Maddie," Sage reluctantly assured her. "He's dangerous."

She looked away, trying to piece all of her fears together into something she could comprehend. Finally, she summoned up the courage to ask the question she already knew he answer to. "He doesn't know, does he? I mean Cord. He doesn't, does he?"

Sage responded with a simple shake of his head, the grim reality in his expression saying more than mere words ever could. Again, she stared off into nothingness, not sure where to go from here. She had feared this and yet here it was. She had never been around bounty hunters before, but she knew of their reputations, nonetheless. Since she had come out west there had been stories floating around about them, what they did and the lengths that they would go to in order to bring someone in who was wanted. They were a ruthless bunch, individuals that she had no interest in having dealings with. And yet, they were after the man that she loved. She didn't know how to process such reality. She wished she didn't have to learn.

"Maddie, it's not safe for you here," Sage finally admitted, though she had already reached that conclusion. "They'll try to get to him through you."

"But I don't have anywhere else to go," she professed, trying to keep her voice down from her sister-in-law hearing her. "Besides, I need to be here for Bree and the baby."

"When is her husband coming home?"

"He's supposed to be back sometime tomorrow."

"Then pack some of your things and be ready to go tomorrow. Just bring what you'll need for a week or so," Sage advised her calmly. "I'll come out tomorrow afternoon and get you. You can stay at my place until all of this is over."

"What do I tell Bree and Kyle? They're going to wonder why I'm leaving. I don't want to lay all of this on them, they have enough to worry about on their own without me piling my problems on top of everything else, but at the same time I also can't lie to them."

"You have to tell them the truth, Maddie," Sage insisted. "They need to know exactly what's going on and what they might have to deal with. It isn't fair to them to leave them out in the dark not knowing if this bounty hunter is going to just show up here. And if he does we don't know what this man is capable of and we sure don't want to find out like that. They deserve to know so they can protect themselves. Kyle is a good man, but he's not a fighter. And you have to think about Bree, not to mention the baby. You'd be putting all of them in harm's way. No, you have to tell them."

"Sage, when will all of this be over?" she asked as if she were looking for the truth. Sage looked over at her, wondering what he should actually tell her the truth. He felt as if she deserved to hear it.

"When Abel Prentiss is dead."

Madeline stared intently at him to see his reaction. "Don't you mean Cord?"

CHAPTER SIXTEEN

After leaving from his talk with Maddie, Cord had headed towards the place that he called home. The Walking A ranch.

As he neared the arch at the entrance to the ranch, he felt more at ease than he had in several days. It always felt good to be back there, to see his friends that he worked with and to see his boss, Joden Gallagher, who had been more of a father-figure to him than his own, drunken excuse for a father had. Gallagher had taken him in and given him a home. But so much more than that, Gallagher had given him purpose.

Cord had spent many years living off the back of a horse, drifting from town to town, either breaking his back herding cattle for a saddle tramp's wages or wondering where his next meal would come from when he wasn't. It was no kind of life to lead and its inconsistencies and uncertainties had grown weary rather quickly. By the time Cord had reached the ripe old age of twenty-five, he had spent as much time in a saddle than out of it. At the time, he had been working for a friend of his, Joden Gallagher, for several years, but being young and restless he began to feel as if he were missing out on some-thing and chose to leave in good terms with the man to chase an elusion. It wasn't long before he realized he had made a huge mistake.

Trying to save face, he tried to make it elsewhere but it just wasn't the same for him. He had almost given up on ever finding his place in the world until he broke down and wired his friend asking for his old job back. It just so happened that Gallagher's ranch was growing and he was looking for ranch hands and offered to give Cord one of the positions. It had come at the perfect time in his life. Although it was yet another job punching cattle, Joden Gallagher made him feel as if he belonged there which, to Cord, was worth its weight in gold.

The quarter horse trotted up the remainder of the road towards the main house as Cord scanned the front of the bunkhouse for his friends. Only a couple of men were hanging around out front and motioned to Cord once he was close enough that they recognized him. He continued on until he had reached the hitching post in front of Joden Gallagher's expansive home. Sliding out of the saddle, he tied off the quarter horse and walked up to the front door. A loud knock brought Joden Gallagher to answer it.

"Cord!" Gallagher responded with a wide, genuine smile as he offered his hand to Cord. "Come on in. What happened to you?" Gallagher spoke as he stepped to the side to allow Cord access into his home. "I was expecting you back yesterday," he added as he closed the door and faced him. "Is everything all right?"

Cord looked at the man, not wanting to lie to him, but also not wanting to cause him unnecessary worry, either.

"I'm sorry about that, Mr. Gallagher," Cord started. "Something unexpected came up."

"Well, you're here now, " Joden Gallagher responded as he turned and stretched out his arm in a welcoming fashion towards the living room. "Come on in. Have a seat and we'll talk about it." Cord followed the man over and took a seat on the leather couch while Gallagher took the high-backed leather chair across from it. Once they were both seated, Gallagher commenced with the discussion.

When he saw Cord's face Gallagher's expression had fallen from one of relief to more of one of concern. "What's going on, Cord? It's not like you not to show up for work."

"Yessir, I know, and I apologize for that, Mr. Gallagher. I just had something come up."

"Is everything alright, Cord?"

"Yessir, I just need to take care of something important, that's all. I was hoping I could take a few more days off to do that. If it's going to put you in an imposition then I understand. I want you to believe that I can still pull my weight around here, but if I've caused you to lose faith in me then I'll understand. I can clear my stuff out of the bunkhouse. I promise, Mr. Gallagher, there won't be any hard feelings."

Cord could tell from Gallagher's reaction that the admission clearly caught the man by surprise. "That's not necessary, Cord. You know I put a lot of faith in you and I know that I can trust you. You're one of my top hands. It's fine if you need some time off, Cord, and you don't have to leave unless you want to, that is."

"No sir," Cord chimed in, "I don't want to. I just didn't want to put you in a bad spot, that's all."

Joden Gallagher's expression turned even more serious. "You're not in some kind of trouble, are you, Cord?"

Cord hesitated, hoping his stall in answering wouldn't give Gallagher more cause to suspect something. He wasn't sure how to answer truthfully without giving the man more to worry about than he deserved. "It's just some things from my past that I need to resolve."

"Oh, I see," Gallagher responded. "Sometimes a man's past catches up with him and he has to face old demons. I just hope it's something you can handle, son," he added with an understanding nod before a thought occurred to him. "Say, does this have anything to do with that big man that came here looking for you this morning?"

The comment caught Cord off guard. *Someone came here? Who would be looking for him? And how did they know to come to the ranch?*

"Who was looking for me?" Cord asked while trying to fake his best surprised look.

"Some fella came out this morning. Great big fella. Maybe the biggest I've ever seen. Said he was a friend of yours."

The thought of who it could be both puzzled Cord and worried him. He had so few friends and this man had claimed to be one of them. He racked his brain trying to think of someone who would have known where to find him, but there wasn't anyone that he was aware of, especially someone who fit that description. The only one that he briefly considered was Nathan, but Joden Gallagher would have mentioned if the man had been black. That only left one possibility: bounty hunter. The idea of such was almost unbelievable. *How could a bounty hunter have gotten wind of him this fast? These things took time, or at least a little longer than he had been missing. That meant that there was a price on his head. Bounty hunters didn't work for free.* Then it came to him. *Judge Hess. Yes, he could have arranged this. He wanted Cord in jail so he could hang him. He could put a man on him this quickly and he wouldn't have to worry about it raising any suspicion.* Cord tried not to react too heavily on the subject.

"Did he say when he was coming back?" he asked.

"No," Joden Gallagher answered innocently. "No, he just said he had been looking for you and wanted to meet up with you. Do you know who it might be?"

Cord nodded. "Yessir, I think so."

"Well, maybe he'll meet up with you soon."

Cord stood and shook hands with Gallagher. "Yessir, I'm sure he will."

After polite pleasantries were exchanged Cord left the Gallagher house and walked over to the bunkhouse to retrieve some of his things when he saw Tell Witherspoon among the ranch hands. He hadn't seen the young man since the last cattle drive going to Hurley when he had found out about River being in town. Tell's face lit up when he saw Cord walk into their midst. Cord passed acknowledgements to the other hands until he caught up with Tell.

"How ya' doin', Cord?" Tell greeted him with a firm handshake and a grin plastered over his face.

"I'm good, Tell. How are things here?"

"Y'know, about the same. How exciting can ranch life be?" Tell sneered with a chuckle. "So, where have you been?"

"Oh, I had some things to take care of," Cord answered nonchalantly as he stuffed the items he had come for into a bag. Tell picked up on the hidden tension in his face.

"Are you sure everything's okay?" Tell asked, his expression softening from concern.

"Yeah, it's fine. Listen, I'm going to be gone for a few days so you try to stay out of trouble."

"Okay, well I guess I'll see you in a few days."

Cord grabbed his bag and threw a wave at the young man as he walked towards the door. "Hopefully, you will," he said under his breath.

Abel Prentiss held the rock tightly in his grasp while slowly sliding the blade of his hunting knife down it in a careful, methodical motion, the scraping sound it made resonating off of the canyon walls that surrounded him. The sun glistened off of the ten-inch blade highlighting it's massive size to where it appeared even larger than it was.

In his line of work as a bounty hunter, Prentiss had always preferred a knife and had never really been that proficient with a gun, at least by the normal standards of the times. He had always thought that men put too much stock in using a gun. Anyone could use a gun, whether they were a good shot or not they were bound to hit something with it just by aiming in the general direction. But a knife was exact. There was no room for error. It had to be right on target or it was ineffective. That's why he had always preferred a knife because it allowed him to get close to his targets which is what he preferred. Using a gun felt like he was allowing the gun to do all of the work for him while a knife made him feel like he had more control. He liked the feeling of knowing that he was responsible for bringing someone down.

Prentiss took a pause, rolling a toothpick in the corner of his mouth with his fingers while watching his reflection in the shiny metal as he slowly turned it back and forth as he considered his next step. He had missed finding Cord Chantry at the ranch, but not by much from what he could gather. Regardless, it wasn't a wasted trip. At least he knew that he was still on the right track. The older man he had talked to there who had said his name was Joden Gallagher had not known where Chantry was at the moment. He had read the man's expression and could tell he was telling the truth. But that didn't matter. He wasn't worried, not in the least. He still had other ways of tracking Cord Chantry down. Just knowing that he was still in the territory was enough to satisfy him, for the time being.

He had patience, something that had served him well in his profession, something that many other bounty hunters he had come across did not have. Not having patience was a detriment to them because when men became impatient, they made mistakes and other people's mistakes were something that helped him. He could capitalize on mistakes because they made his job easier.

When a man is patient he thinks clearer because he isn't pressed for time. Feeling pressured for time also caused people to make mistakes. He had seen it before many times in many situations. A bounty hunter pushing himself and getting caught up so much in being in a hurry to collect a bounty that they were careless. More times than not that way of thinking cost them time and, more importantly, opportunity. Such was not his mindset. He preferred to be patient and do it right the first time He could afford to wait. Wait out his prey. Wait for the right time to make a move.

He could be patient. It was obvious that Cord Chantry wasn't going anywhere so he could afford to wait as long as need be.

Prentiss grinned as he watched his reflection again in the blade.

He didn't care what Judge Hess had to say about it. He would catch Cord Chantry soon, he was sure of it and when he did *he* would decide whether or not he was going to kill him.

A knock on the door alerted Madeline Stafford that Sage had arrived. Her brother, Kyle, had made it back a few hours earlier, giving her just enough time to welcome him back before she was forced to tell him what had transpired. Kyle did not take the news well, as she had expected, his first concern being Bree and the baby. Maddie explained everything as best she could, but it still didn't help that he and his family had possibly been placed in danger. The only good news was that Kyle would not be leaving again and would be around to protect his family. After talking over their options with Maddie they decided to remain in their home and be vigilant watching out for visitors.

Maddie glanced outside to verify that it was, in fact, Sage before she removed the bar and opened the door. "Hey," he spoke to Kyle and Bree who both returned the gesture before turning back to Maddie. "Are you ready?" Sage asked her.

"Yeah. My things are over here," she responded as she picked up her bags and addressed her family as she started for the door. "Bye. I'll see you in about a week or so."

Kyle and Bree said their goodbyes and Sage waved to her family as he closed the door behind her. She brought her bags over to the horse Sage had brought with him and sat them on the ground next to it.

"Sorry I couldn't get a wagon," Sage apologized. "At least its not a long trip into town."

She smiled to deflect her disappointment. "It's fine. Thanks."

"Here, let me help you with those," he said as he grabbed one of the bags and tied it onto his horse and then secured the other bag to her own before looking at her. He saw that she was wearing riding pants, but he still thought it best to offer his help anyway. "Do you need help getting up?" he asked her more out of politeness than concern.

"No, I'm fine," Maddie answered as she stepped up into the stirrup and onto her horse and grabbed the reins with Sage following suit. He pulled his horse in the direction of town and looked over at her one final time. "Ready?" he asked. She nodded without speaking as they started out for the town of Hurley.

The ride was fairly quiet all the way to town with neither one of them knowing exactly what to say that could take the pressure off of what they were being forced to do. Neither of them blamed Cord for the circumstance being what there were, though neither felt the need to express the notion to one another, while, at the same time, both of them wished there had been another solution to the problem. Still, Maddie was grateful to be staying at Sage's home. With it being in the edge of town and with Sage having lost his job it was comforting to know that he would be around to help protect her until the federal marshall could arrive and, hopefully, help smooth all of this out.

By the time they had arrived at Sage's house and moved Maddie's belongings inside, the sun had finished its movement for the day and it was a shade before dark. Maddie settled into her room while Sage whipped up fried potatoes to go along with some jerky he had been saving. After eating amidst idle small talk, the two sat on the front porch sipping coffee, both of them silently wondering the whereabouts of Cord Chantry.

CHAPTER SEVENTEEN

The crispness of the evening was enough to encourage Cord to throw several more pieces of wood onto the fire. He couldn't tell if the chill he was feeling inside of him was from the evening passing over him without the help of a warming sun or if it was the uncertainty he was now facing. Maybe it was a mixture of both. As he tossed the logs onto the glowing embers he leaned back, allowing the brightly-colored sparkles it created to float into the nighttime air, rising above his head erratically until they cooled enough where they disappeared into the clear, darkened sky.

He leaned back against the underside of his saddle after peeling off another chunk of the rabbit that remained warming over the spit. Along with the beans he had stewed it was the makings of a simple meal, but to him, a man who was accustomed to living off the back of a horse, it felt more like a feast. He tried to enjoy the quiet and solitude that the night brought, realizing it might be the last such shred of peace he would have until all of this was over. What concerned him now was that his thoughts kept going back to the man who had come to the ranch looking for him.

There was no denying it. The man had to be a bounty hunter and if he were bold enough to come out to the ranch looking for him then he was bold enough to do anything to get to him. That meant he, Cord, would have to be on guard all the time and be ready for anything. That also meant that there was only one possible way out of this. He had to bring in Jesse Morse. Morse was the key to this whole situation, a situation that was sure to only worsen without Morse's testimony. But he had tried to get Morse's cooperation before the easy way by trying to reason with him and it had ended badly, almost getting him shot and arrested. Now he had no time for negotiating or hand holding. His days of being nice were over. This man was coming with him back to Hurley one way or another.

There was also something else to consider in all of this: Maddie. If this man was whom he suspected and he turned out to be a bounty hunter, he would stop at nothing to bring Cord in, or kill him. He wasn't quite sure what the man's instructions were, but sooner or later he would eventually find out about Maddie, if he didn't already know. It was feasible. The man had found out about the Walking A ranch. How could he not also find out about Maddie? A wave of panic encircled him as the thought sunk deep into his mind. Maddie would be in danger, if she wasn't already. At least for the time being Jesse Morse would have to wait, even if it meant he never caught up to Morse again and ended up going to jail, or worse. Whatever his fate, that no longer mattered. Right now, his first priority was to make sure Maddie was safe.

That night, Cord's sleep was sporadic and restless, to say the least. He couldn't get the thought of worrying about Maddie's fate out of his mind. He finally rolled out of bed just before dawn and fixed a quick meal before breaking down his camp and saddling the quarter horse just as the sun began to emerge from over the mountains. It would take him most of the morning to make it to her brother's house and he would be on edge until he made it there and saw for himself that she was okay. The only problem was she could no longer stay there. The bounty hunter would find her there, eventually, if he hadn't already. *Stop thinking that way...*

He urged the quarter horse into a gallop, putting as much distance behind him as he thought the animal could take. By his estimates he should be able to make it to Maddie by midday, possibly sooner, he wasn't sure because he wasn't thinking clearly. All he could think about was how he would never forgive himself if something happened to her.

His heart swelled with anticipation when he saw the house coming into sight. There was no sign of horses out in front which was a good sign or so he had to believe. It would do no good to come up to the front of a house in broad daylight if you were trying to stay concealed, he kept telling himself. As he neared the house his horse couldn't get him there fast enough. He made up the last few yards while swinging his leg over the saddle. By the time the horse had come to a stop in front of the hitching rail Cord was already planting his foot onto the ground and quickly walking towards the front door, gun drawn and ready for anything. He knocked on the door holding his gun down by his side out of sight, but still close enough by in case he needed it. He heard the bar on the door being removed and he paused, taking in a tight breath and waited. When the door opened, Bree was standing there. When she saw Cord her tone was calm, but cold.

"Why, hello, Cord," she greeted him without expression. "Maddie isn't here," she offered up quickly.

Cord tried to be patient. "Where is she?"

"She left yesterday afternoon with Sage," she stated firmly

as she crossed her arms, her eyes fixed hard on him. "They were going to his place until all of this is over."

"Okay. Thanks, Bree," he responded, hoping that would be the end of the discussion. He was wrong. When he turned to leave she spoke again, stopping him in his tracks.

"Y'know, Cord, we had to sleep with a gun next to our bed last night. That's the first time we've ever had to do that since we came out west and it's all because of you. All the scary talk about how people out here mistreated new settlers and indian attacks and famine and drought and the harsh weather, none of that scared us as much as this has scared us. None of those things could have been avoided but this could have. That's what's so frustrating in all of this. This was caused by your actions and nothing else. You've put my family into a panic and we can't even enjoy our lives here anymore."

Cord turned back to face her scornful stare. "I know and I'm sorry, Bree. I didn't mean for any of this to happen."

"But it did happen," she continued berating him as she took a step closer. "Maddie told me what you did, how you shot that man even after everyone around you told you to leave it alone. But you wouldn't listen, would you? You had to prove what a big man you were, to exact vengeance and try to right a wrong. Well, you can't undo a bad deed, Cord, it doesn't work that way. I hate what you're doing and what you're planning to do and I hate you for forcing us to live in fear. You had no right bringing this kind of trouble to my home and putting my family at risk. It isn't right, Cord, and it isn't fair. We did nothing to deserve this. It's hard enough trying to make it out here without having something else being thrown at you that wasn't necessary. We don't deserve this. I know Maddie certainly doesn't deserve this, either."

"I'm sorry, Bree," Cord repeated. "You've got to believe me. I really didn't mean for any of this to happen."

Bree took another short step towards Cord, her arms

dropping down by her side in anger. "You didn't mean for it to happen? What did you think was going to happen, Cord? You killed a man. There are consequences to that. There's always going to be consequences when you kill someone."

"But it was self-defense," he tried to explain calmly knowing she was much too emotional now to understand his side of things.

"It doesn't matter if it was self-defense! If you hadn't put yourself in that position you wouldn't have needed to shoot that man. Maddie told me that the man was from the stage-coach incident when she was traveling out here. That was almost a year ago. *A year,* Cord! You didn't feel the need to kill the man in all that time so why all of a sudden was it necessary to do it now?"

"It was the first time I had run into him."

"You mean you hadn't been looking for him all that time?"

"No, I hadn't. I was willing to let it go, but I...I...couldn't."

"What changed all of a sudden?"

"I couldn't let it go. I kept having this nightmare..."

"Oh, so you killed a man because you had a nightmare."

"He killed a man, Bree," Cord blurted out as he continued to try to argue his side. "A young man. A friend of mine."

"I'm sorry for your friend, Cord, but that still doesn't make it right. There's always going to be killings. That's what I hate about living out here. Everything is guns, guns, guns. People can't resolve an issue without using a gun. Everything revolves around guns. There's so much killing and there'll always be more killing because men can only solve a disagreement by using a gun."

"Bree, I'm sorry."

The apology seemed to have distinguished some of her anger, at least he wanted more than anything to believe that. Her expression and her tone slightly softened as she began to calm down from her release. "I am, too, Cord. I just hope

Maddie can see through all of this and understand what she's getting herself into. I don't wish you any harm, Cord, really I don't, but at the same time I don't agree with your actions, either. I hope you understand." With that she turned and stepped back into the house and closed the door. As Cord turned to walk to his horse he heard the bar being placed on the back of the door reminding him that their fear and being forced to live on the edge was all his fault.

He climbed into his saddle and turned the quarter horse towards Benton Springs, his mind fixed in concentration. Hearing that Sage had Maddie with him was a relief. At least while she was with him she wouldn't be in danger, leaving him to focus on the task at hand which was to find Jesse Morse and bring him in. The first place he would try would be the hotel where he had confronted him the last time. As far as the sheriff and Jesse Morse were concerned Cord had left town for good, at least he hoped that was their belief. If he were going to make this work he would have to work fast and be ready to move on a moment's notice. Snatching Morse would not be easy. The kid now knew that Cord was after him and Cord hoped that the kid not seeing him around since their meeting and having had the sheriff intervene would give the kid a false sense of security. That would be the only thing on Cord's side in all of this.

It was late afternoon just before it started getting dark when Cord's horse walked into Benton Springs. The streets were deserted except for an occasional individual leaving a saloon in a subdued, slightly inebriated state staggering down the boardwalk to sleep off their good times somewhere in a bed. He continued on through town till he came to the hotel where he had confronted Morse. Splitting the buildings he walked the quarter horse between them and around to the back and tied it off. He glanced around in the shadows looking for movement of any kind, but seeing none he went up the stairs and inside the back door. He would try the same room where he had previously found Morse, just on the chance that he had remained there.

Cord walked the short distance to room seven, the room where he had confronted Morse before, removing his trigger guard as he did. He paused at the door taking in a deep breath to ready himself and then knocked. He heard footsteps inside the room. A few tense seconds later, the door opened.

CHAPTER EIGHTEEN

When the door opened, Cord was staring at a man he had never seen before. The man could see Cord's disappointment showing through in his expression as he gave Cord a puzzled look in return. "Can I help you?" the man asked hesitantly.

Cord stood motionless for a second until it hit him that Jesse Morse was gone. "Uh...no, no sir, I'm sorry. I was looking for someone else. Sorry to bother you." The man nodded and slowly closed the door, leaving Cord standing in the hallway wondering what his next move would be. He was already tired of chasing this man down. Right now he didn't have the patience for it and he didn't have the time for it. Nor did Maddie, for that matter. The reality was the longer it took him to bring Jesse Morse in, the longer Maddie would be in danger. He had to change the way he was looking for Morse.

Cord decided to go over to the livery stables first and check for Morse's horse. He remembered the description Tom Wills had gotten from the hotel clerk in Hurley: tan mustang, large white patch on its right side. He would start with that. It made sense that if the horse was still at the stables then it meant Jesse Morse was still in town. He left the hotel headed for the stables.

When Cord got to the stalls, he met up with the stable owner who was busy giving hay to the animals. The man stopped working and looked up when he saw Cord coming in. "Can I help you?" he asked while leaning on his pitchfork.

"I'm here to get my friend's horse," Cord said with a casual smile. "We're heading out of town and he's getting some supplies from the general store. He asked me to bring it over there to him."

The stable owner eyed Cord carefully. Cord couldn't tell by his expression whether or not the man was believing him. "What's your friend's name?"

"Jesse Morse. He's a little younger then me, about this tall," Cord motioned with his hand five or six inches shorter than himself, "brown hair, tan vest and pants, dark blue shirt and a black Hardee hat. He rides a tan mustang that has a large white spot on its right side."

The description caused the stable owner's expression to soften a little showing Cord that he was winning over the man's trust. Cord tried to maintain his composure and not act suspicious, but he felt exposed being in such a public place. And what if Morse came looking for his horse before he had a chance to get out of there with it? The territory hanged horse thieves. If they discovered that he was a fraud, he was done for. There would be no way he could make it out of town without being pursued by the law, or worse, a posse.

"How come you didn't come into town with him?" the stable owner asked, testing his response.

"I was meeting him here. I've spent the last three weeks on a cattle drive. We were supposed to meet up and head back to the ranch."

"What's the name of the ranch?"

"The Walking A," Cord said without hesitation.

The owner continued studying him closely. Finally, he made his decision. "You owe me a dollar for the boarding and another dollar for the feed."

Cord smiled as he fished the coins from his pocket and dropped them into the stable owner's open palm. The stable owner nodded with his head towards the other end of the barn. "He's right over there," the owner obliged as he walked Cord over to one of the far stalls. Standing there eating a bucket of oats was a tan mustang. Cord walked around to the right side of the animal and saw the large white patch. This was definitely Jesse Morse's horse.

"That's him," Cord said as he picked the saddle up from off of the railing and began saddling him. The stable owner walked back and continued dividing out hay as Cord finished with the saddle. He led the horse out, tossing the stable owner a wave and a nod as he walked Jesse Morse's horse out into the street. Now, came the hard part.

Jesse Morse was somewhere in Benton Springs, but so was Sheriff Nix and his men, whom he had already had a run-in with, not to mention a possible bounty hunter. The only thing going for him was the unlikelihood that there were wanted posters circulating with his likeness on them. The trick was going to be finding Jesse Morse and bringing him back to Hurley while trying to dodge Sheriff Nix and his deputy while also keeping a distance from this bounty hunter. His searching would have to be quick for if Morse managed to slip out of town while Cord was searching for him he'd likely never run across the man again and he, Cord, would have to spend the rest of his life on the run.

Cord tied off his horse at the opposite end of town from the sheriff's office and started his search, glancing inside building after building hoping for a glimpse of Morse, but by the time he had covered the west end of town he had had no luck. He turned and started back down the opposite side of

the street, taking his time to avoid suspicion from the townspeople and trying his best to blend in as much as possible.
His only choice now was to search the other end of town,
where the sheriff's office was located.

Once he had sufficiently covered the other side of the
street, Cord took his horse and walked it back behind the
buildings to avoid possibly being spotted by the sheriff.
When he had made it to the east end of town he turned the
corner and casually walked the quarter horse over to the first
hitching post. When he dismounted, he scanned the buildings trying to eliminate as many as he could that he didn't feel
he needed to search. It was best if he was only on the streets
as long as necessary. The longer he was visible the more likely
it was that he would be spotted. The problem was he was
running out of places that Morse could be.

He inventoried what buildings were left: a general store,
two saloons, a barber shop, a bath house and the freight
office. Morse wouldn't have any freight to handle so that one
was out and judging from the boyish face he remembered the
man having it was likely that he was too young to need a
shave. That left the bath house, general store and two
saloons. Since he needed a few things before he left town, he
decided to try the general store first using the purchase to
cover his presence.

Cord walked over to the store and went inside. He picked
up some coffee and more jerky as he looked around for Jesse
More, but he was nowhere in sight. After paying for the
items, he walked them back out to his horse and stuffed them
into his saddlebags before heading to the bath house while
leading the two horses. He tied them off and walked up
behind a man who was walking around between the divided
tents handing out clean towels.

"I'd like a bath," Cord announced to the man, causing him
to turn and face Cord.

"Why, certainly, sir," the man happily responded with a broad smile. "Would you like hot water, too? It's only twenty-five cents more?"

"Cold will be fine," Cord assured him. He could see a flake of disappointment in the man's eyes, but it was short lived.

"Very well. Right this way," the man said as he renewed his smile and led Cord down through the tents towards one that was open. As they passed the other tents, Cord sneaked a peek inside each of them to see if Jesse Morse was anywhere to be seen. At the third tent, Cord spotted who he thought to be Morse sitting in a tub. His quick glance caused him to stop and take a step back to make sure it was him. It was. He walk swiftly and caught up with the owner just as he was pulling back a sheet to show Cord the tub he would be using. Cord took a step in as the owner closed the sheet behind him. "Here you are."

Cord hesitated. "You don't happen to use Lye soap, do you?"

"Why, yessir, we do. Made right here on the premises," the owner said with a prideful smile.

"I'm allergic to Lye," Cord tried to explain. "Gives me welts. Makes me look like I was dragged through a prickly pear bush."

"Oh, dear."

"Yeah, I can't do that."

"Well, I'm afraid it's all we have at the moment."

"Maybe I'll check with you next time. Thanks." Cord said as he walked back towards the front and over to the side with the horses. He was out of sight behind several trees, but he could still keep an eye on movement in and out of the bath house. He stood under the trees for a little while watching customers coming and going until he finally saw Jesse Morse appear, adjusting his gun belt as he left walking into town. Cord quickly climbed into his saddle and pulled Morse's horse as he went around the back of the bath tents. He skirted the tents and came up between the freight office, a stand alone structure and the wall of the first building of town, stopping some thirty feet back between the two. He climbed down from his horse and drew his gun as he walked up to the edge of the freight office while waiting with his back against the wall.

Cord heard Morse's footsteps as he glanced down into town once more to make sure no one was immediately around them. When Morse passed by him Cord stepped out and struck him on the back of the head with his gun. An unconscious Morse started to fall, but Cord caught him. He holstered his gun and threw the young man over his shoulder and walked him back to his horse, sliding him over his saddle and grabbing the reins before climbing onto his own horse and leading the two out of town towards Hurley.

Jesse Morse squinted as he tried to open his eyes in the glaring sun. Before he could determine exactly where he was he felt the stabbing sensation of his headache taking over his thoughts. He tried shaking his head gently to try to rid it of the fogginess but it didn't work. Only when he tried to raise his hand to cup his head in it did he realize that his hands were tied to the pommel of his saddle. His thoughts suddenly cleared as he tried to yank his hands free of the rope, but couldn't.

"Don't waste your time," Cord said calmly. "If there's one thing I've learned from handling cattle its how to tie a good knot."

Jesse Morse glanced over at Cord who was riding beside him holding the reins to Morse's horse. Morse flew into a fit of rage and began pulling at his hands with all of his strength as he gritted his teeth in anger. After unsuccessfully freeing himself he leaned his head back and let out a deafening scream of defeat as his body shook.

"Yell your head off, if you want," Cord responded to the call. "Ain't nobody around to hear you."

Morse looked around him and saw that they were out in the country with nothing around them. He quickly spun in his saddle to look behind them and saw nothing of Benton Springs. Enraged, Morse turned back to Cord.

"Let me go!" He shouted.

"I told you that you were coming back to Hurley with me one way or another. You could have made it easy or you could have chose to be hard about it. You picked the hard way."

"I'm not testifying so let me go!"

Cord ignored the threat.

"I'll tell 'em I didn't see anything!"

"Then I'll bring the bartender in as a witness. He's already told me you were there next to the man I shot. That places you right there where his gun dropped when you picked it up."

"I don't care! I won't tell them anything!"

"You won't have to, kid. When the bartender places you there next to the dead man you won't have any choice but to tell the truth. The judge will see to that."

CHAPTER NINETEEN

The sun had just clipped the peaks of the mountains as it began to tuck itself away for the night. There was no movement in town, at least none that Sage Connelly could see from his front porch. He had a clear line of sight to the livery stables some fifty yards away, but nothing much really beyond that. Still, it was nice to live on the outskirts of town, even if he was no longer responsible for keeping it safe.

As the chill of the rapidly cooled air started to pass over him Sage polished off the last few drops of his tepid coffee and decided to go inside for the night. Maddie had been cooking that evening and had whipped up an apple pie which she had strategically placed on the breakfast table to cool. She had also conveniently left a knife and a plate next to it just on the chance that Sage might like to cut himself a slice. As he opened the front door, the waft of the pie cascaded over him, reminding him of the treat that awaited him. He stepped in, licking his lips, his taste buds exploding with sensation in anticipation. He had closed the door behind him and was releasing the doorknob when the door suddenly flung open with such force that it knocked him onto the floor. He immediately turned around to see Abel Prentiss standing in the doorway.

Compared to Sage's five-foot-ten frame the man was massive, his sheer size catching Sage by surprise, not to mention the obvious shock of his sudden appearance. He slid across the floor with his hands behind him and pushing off with his legs to put distance between them. Prentiss casually closed the door behind him without looking and stood there, a devious grin spread over his face.

"Well, you must be the ex-sheriff," Prentiss bellowed in his deep voice as he took a short step towards Sage who was still sliding backwards in retreat while watching him. Sage stopped sliding when he felt the back of his head bump into the kitchen table. Just then, Madeline appeared in the doorway of the bedroom directly behind him to check on what had made the noise. When she saw the large man, she screamed.

"Hello there, pretty lady. I see your wife wants in on the fun," Prentiss said as he took another short step towards Sage and then another. Sage started trying to get up without taking his eyes off of the man. He leveled his eyes at the big man as he made it to his feet.

"Maddie?" Sage calmly spoke. "Run."

That was when Abel Prentiss made his move.

Sage was shocked at how quickly he moved for a man his size. He had only taken a few steps when he was on Sage. Sage braced himself and swung a hard right and caught Prentiss squarely on the jaw, barely turning his head atop his thick neck without even moving his body. Prentiss slowly turned his eyes back to Sage and grinned.

Prentiss threw a left jab at Sage before grabbing Sage's shirt and following it up with a staggering right to the side of his face. The blow caught Sage on the jaw snapping his head around as if he had been kicked by a horse. He felt his senses misfiring as he tried to regain his composure before Prentiss landed a shot to his gut, folding him over and abruptly forcing the air out of his lungs. Prentiss released his grip on Sage's shirt and allowed him to plummet onto his knees as Sage's lungs desperately fought to breath. Prentiss was reaching down to collect Sage when Maddie walked up to him and hit him in the head with the plate lying on the table. The move only managed to anger Prentiss.

He pulled his hand back and slapped Maddie with the back of it, the sharp sound of it connecting with her face filled the room as Maddie flew backwards onto the floor, stunned so harshly that she was barely able to move. Sage took the opportunity of Prentiss being distracted to pick up a chair and swing it with all of his strength at Prentiss' back. The chair shattered over his wide shoulders, causing him to lean forward, but only briefly, not delivering as much effect as Sage had hoped. As he stood back up, Prentiss swung the back of his hand up against Sage's face, the momentum and the force throwing Sage's head back so far that he almost lost his footing. Prentiss hit him with a clubbing right, a left to his ribs and then another crashing right to the side of his skull. As Sage's legs begin to give out from under him from the horrific beating, he tasted the coppery bitterness of his own blood flowing from the numerous open wounds around his mouth.

The powerful blows had taken a heavy toll on him, his head weaving about as he desperately tried to steady it, but without success. His balance was failing and his vision was becoming distorted. Prentiss had delivered a massive amount of damage to Sage, forcing him to wonder how much more his injured body could take. Try as he may he couldn't force his mind to think clearly. He could feel the front of his shirt becoming wet, but he couldn't distinguish if it was from sweat or blood or both.

He stumbled forward, reeling from the punches and swinging blindly. With his left eye almost completely closed from the brutal attack, he swung wildly, hoping to find his mark, but missing. His body half slumped over, his face was drawn and his eyes sagging as he was no longer able to close his mouth as the thin stream of fresh blood dripped from it and onto the floor. Prentiss abandoned Sage and started towards Maddie, but Sage mustered his last bit of resilience and grabbed Prentiss by the shirt to stop him. He had pulled his fist back to swing when Prentiss swung around and caught Sage with a devastating right punch to the side of his head, dropping Sage onto the floor like a rag doll.

Still partially incoherent, Sage was combining ever last bit of strength that he could gather to force his arms underneath his body to try to push himself up off of the floor when he felt Prentiss' massive hands grab him and jerk him to his feet without him using his own legs. The man's strength was unbelievable. Holding Sage with his left hand, Prentiss delivered a staggering right, then another, then another before he fired a devastating blow to Sage's gut. Sage cried out in agony from several ribs breaking. He then gripped Sage's shirt and swung wide striking Sage in the jaw. The blow was so lethal that Sage was physically crippled as Prentiss released his grip and allowed the man's limp body to drop to the floor.

Sage found himself lying on his stomach facing Maddie. He could barely make out through his swollen eye that she was still barely conscious. He tried with all his might to move towards her, but his body refused to respond. His breathing was raspy from his neck being slammed to the side from the tremendous abuse he had endured to his head. He tried to speak, but his jaw would not cooperate. His breathing was coming in short, labored bursts from the immense pressure in his chest. All he could do was watch helplessly as Prentiss walked over to Maddie, turning back to look down at Sage as the devious grin appeared back on his face.

The last thing he heard before he passed out was Maddie screaming.

It was just growing dark when Cord led Jesse Morse's horse into the town of Hurley. The streets were virtually deserted except for a stray dog who paused on the side of the street to allow the two horses to pass, folding his ears back and wagging his tail at them as a friendly gesture in the hopes of garnishing some attention.

Cord led them over to the sheriff's office. He had planned on not reaching town until after sundown hoping that there would not be anyone around to harass him. He had no idea where the bounty hunter was at the moment, but he felt confident that the man wouldn't be hanging around town in the dark on the chance that Cord would simply show up.

He climbed down and tied off both horses before walking over to Jesse's horse. He caught the young man's hateful stare as he approached him. "I'm going to untie you. Don't try anything or I'll snatch your butt off that horse and onto the ground. Got it?"

Morse nodded, none too pleased with the threat or the direction things were going. Cord pulled out his pocketknife and sliced the ropes away from Morse's hands. Morse freed himself of the pieces of rope and took a few seconds to rub the irritation and stiffness caused by the ropes from his wrists. As Cord was putting away his knife, Morse kicked him in the chest and kicked the sides of his horse to try to get it to run, but before he could Cord reached up and grabbed him by the shirt and pulled him off of the horse and swung around tossing him flat onto the ground. Morse gave out a painful grunt as he landed on his back. He laid there barely able to move as Cord turned to look down at him. "Thought I was kidding, didn't 'ya?" He reached down and grabbed Morse by the neck of his shirt and jerked him to his feet.

Cord walked Morse inside the sheriff's office and forced him into a chair. "Hey!" Morse resounded from the rough handling.

"Stay there." Cord instructed him with a pointed finger as he pulled out a match and lit the lantern. Once the glow filled the room he stepped over to the desk and retrieved the cell keys from the drawer. The jingling of the keys alerted Morse to what Cord had planned. His face went flush with worry.

"Wait...what are you doing?"

"Come on, let's go," Cord insisted.

"Are you locking me up? You can't be serious."

"Let's go," Cord repeated as he grabbed Morse by the arm and helped lift him out of the chair. As Morse was getting to his feet he struggled to free himself from Cord's grip. "No, I'm not going in a cell. Stop! I'm not going!"

"Stop whining and move," Cord tried to move the young man, but he pulled back to try to get away.

"No! I told you, I'm not getting locked up!"

Cord's patience had reached its limit. He grabbed Morse by the shirt and pulled him towards him, almost lifting him off of his feet. He stared at the young man with his piercing light grey eyes. "I told you I was bringing you in to testify, but I didn't say what kind of condition you'd be in." Morse's face went blank from the threat as Cord did not waiver. "Now, get in the cell."

When Cord released him Morse's expression was still one of shock as he slowly walked ahead of Cord and into the waiting cell. Cord closed the metal door behind him and locked it, tossing him one last icy stare before walking out of the outer cell door and closing it. He tossed the keys back into the desk drawer and blew out the lantern. As he walked out onto the boardwalk and was closing the outside door of the sheriff's office, he heard Morris yell, "what about supper?"

CHAPTER TWENTY

When Cord left the sheriff's office he decided to head over to Sage Connelly's house and see Maddie. He had some explaining to do to her and he didn't want to have to wait any longer to get everything out in the open. He longed for the day when all of this would be over and they could get back to planning their future together.

The walk to Sage's house was a short one, but Cord decided to bring Sage's quarter horse with him so he could swap it out with his buckskin. Even though the quarter horse had been a good reliable animal he had grown quite accustomed to the mannerisms and traits of his own horse. He had also brought Morse's horse to leave at Sage's house until he could get it over to the livery stables. He had no idea how long Morse would be in jail so he though it best to at least care for the animal till such time as the federal marshall could make it to town. He would need to go to see Tom Wills first thing in the morning to inform him who Jesse Morse was and why he was locked up.

Cord turned the corner at the last building in town and

headed towards Sage's house. As he neared it, he felt as if something was out of place. There was a light on inside the house, but the front door had been left partially open, something that seemed quite out of character for someone as neat and tidy as Sage. The closer to the house that Cord was the less he liked what he was seeing.

When he had made it to the hitching rail he paused and listened. There was no sound coming from the house, no one sitting on the front porch drinking coffee as was customary for Sage this time of the evening. There wasn't even the aroma of coffee having been brewed. Cord continued staring at the house as he dismounted and tied off the horses. "Sage?" he called out, but there was no answer. *Somethings not right.* He pulled his gun and started for the front door.

With each careful step Cord strained his ears to listen, but he still heard no movement of any kind coming from inside of the house. "Sage?" he paused for an answer. "Maddie?" he listened again. Nothing.

When he had made it up to the front porch he tried to look inside the window, but the curtains blocked some of his vision. He moved over to the door and paused. No sounds inside. He slowly pushed the door the rest of the way open with his left hand, his gun firmly grasped in his right. When it had swung open wide enough he saw him.

"Sage!" he holstered his gun and hurriedly walked over to Sage who was laying unconscious face down on the floor next to the table. Cord felt for a pulse in his neck and found only a faint, weak heartbeat. He carefully turned Sage over onto his back and was taken back by the man's appearance. His face was almost unrecognizable from the horrific beating he had endured. His face was distorted and swollen almost to the point that he could barely breathe from his broken nose. As he struggled to take in air, his breathing was gruff and cracked and each time Sage took in a breath Cord could hear rattling coming from his throat. He wanted to move him, but feared what kind of internal damage he might have endured and thought it best not to do so. Cord leaned down closer to the man's mangled face next to his ear.

"Sage," Cord whispered softly as he gingerly shook his shoulder. The sound and movement jarred Sage's body as his one good eye flew open wide from the shock. His breathing became sporadic as he began hyperventilating from fear. His raspy voice was having trouble forming words as Cord patted his shoulder gently, while Sage continued staring blindly up at the ceiling. "Sage, it's me, Cord," he once again tried reassuring him. Finally, Sage's head slowly turned enough that his good eye could see Cord's face. It wasn't instantly that he recognized Cord, but when he did, his mouth began struggling trying to speak, but all Cord could hear was gravelly hoarseness.

Cord spoke softly as he continued to hold his hand on Sage's shoulder. "Sage, who did this to you?"

Sage's mouth was moving but Cord was having difficulty hearing him. He leaned down closer with his ear up next to Sage's mouth. "Boun...boun...bounty..."

"*Bounty?*" Cord finished the word for him. "*Bounty hunter?* Did the bounty hunter do this?" he asked while looking for a reaction. Sage slowly and gradually nodded.

"Sage, where's Maddie? Where's Maddie? Is Maddie here?"

Sage nodded again as he tried to answer him. "Bed...bedroom."

Cord looked up and saw that the door to one of the bedrooms was closed. He imagined the worst.

He jumped up and ran over to the door and opened it, his mouth falling open from the shock at what he saw. Maddie was lying on the floor on her side in a crumpled pile, her hair tossed about and stringy. She was not moving. "Maddie!" he shouted as he went over to her. When his hand touched her arm, she recoiled and screamed, her entire body shaking as she continued screaming and trying to get away from him. He kept calling her name over and over as he tried to get her to make eye contact with him so that she could see that he wasn't the bounty hunter. It took several attempts to convince her to face him and even when she did her recognition of who he was wasn't instant. Finally, her expression changed and she realize that it was Cord. She grabbed him and squeezed him tightly as she began to sob uncontrollably. Cord had to confront her until she was able to calm down enough for him to get a good look at her. When he did, he was shocked and disturbed by her appearance.

Her left eye was already blackened and completely closed from the beating, her mouth swollen horribly. Her lip was split in several places and dried blood caked her cheek and had been so severe that it had managed to run all the way down her chin and neck and onto the top portion of her dress. His right wrist was badly bruised which led Cord to believe that it had occurred from the bounty hunter grabbing it tightly so she couldn't get away as he held onto her to beat her. Judging from the shape and distortion of it there was a good chance that her nose was broken.

He held her in his arms as her entire body shook from the trauma of being savagely beaten. Even after she had calmed her crying she still refused to let him go as she collapsed into him for protection. Despite her injuries being severe, Sage's wounds were unfortunately much worse. At first, he considered taking him with them, but he was afraid he wasn't sure just how bad his injuries were and he didn't want to risk making things worse- much worse. But he had to, regardless. He knew if he didn't get him to a doctor soon he would surely die. In fact, he might not make it even if he did. Cord was finally forced to tell her what he had dreaded. "Maddie? I need to go get the doctor," he announced as her hold on him intensified. "Maddie, you and Sage need a doctor." Again, she clamped down her hold on him.

He took her by the shoulders and carefully pulled her back away from him so he could look into her eyes. "Maddie? I know you're scared, but if I don't get a doctor for Sage soon he isn't going to make it." Her face distorted from crying.

"Maddie, I need you to listen to me. Sage is hurt really bad. He needs a doctor, now. I can't wait. Do you hear what I'm saying? If I don't get him to a doctor soon he's going to die. Do you want to go with me or stay here?"

Maddie shook her head, but was unable to speak.

Cord was having to get more stern with her. Sage didn't have time to wait. "Maddie, I have to go. Are you coming with me? " She shook her head again. His voice got even more stern. "Maddie, Sage will die. Are you coming with me? Yes or no?"

When she looked into his eyes he felt sorry for making her have to choose, but he had no choice in the matter. She finally nodded in agreement. "You're coming with me?"

She nodded.

He helped her to her feet and they hurried out into the front room where Sage lay. Cord bent over and checked Sage's pulse. Very weak. He grabbed Sage under the arms ad pulled him out the door and over to the horses. It took some effort but he was finally able to put Sage up onto Jesse Morse's horse. He helped Maddie onto his horse and climbed behind Sage and held onto him. He glanced over at Maddie. "Are you okay to ride?"

She nodded yes.

Cord pulled the reins and they started heading towards Doc Ballen's office.

· · ·

They pulled up at the doctor's office and Cord jumped down and helped Sage down from the saddle as Maddie dismounted and waited. Cord carried Sage up to the door and kicked it repeatedly with his boot as he waited for the light inside to appear. Through the window he saw a faint glow becoming brighter and brighter as someone came from the back and into the front office. Doc Ballen looked out the window at them before they heard the door unlock and open.

As soon as the door opened, Cord carried Sage inside.

"What happened to him?" Doc Ballen asked was he quickly closed the door and led them towards the examination room with Cord right behind him.

"He's been beaten" Cord informed him as he started to lay Sage on the table.

"Careful," Doc Ballen told him as he helped lower his head onto the table. Doc Ballen glanced up at Maddie and noticed her injuries and started to say something, but she shook her head and pointed down at Sage. Doc Ballen looked over at Cord and then back to Maddie and nodded in acknowledgement before going back to work on Sage. Cord and Maddie stood over the opposite end of the table for the first few minutes and watched him examine Sage before Doc Ballen finally spoke.

"Is *this* Sheriff Connelly?" Doc Ballen asked.

"Yeah."

"It's hard to tell. I didn't get a good look at him until now." He started working on Sage and then paused. "Why don't you two go sit in the waiting room. I might be awhile." Cord hesitated. "Please," Doc Ballen asked as he looked at Cord again. "As soon as I get him stable I'll take a look at you, my dear." Cord finally nodded and walked towards the waiting room, while holding on to Maddie. They sat and Maddie leaned her head onto Cord's chest as he wrapped his arm around her and pulled her closer.

This was the second time a friend of his had been seriously hurt because of him. He was worried about Sage. He did not want to leave one of his only friends alone. A friend that had been seriously beaten because of him.

A friend that might very likely die.

CHAPTER TWENTY-ONE

He didn't know just how long they had been asleep when Doc Ballen shook his shoulder to wake him, but judging from the sweat and wear on the man's face, it had been a considerable amount of time. Cord stirred, quickly wiping the sleep away from his eyes and stood as the doctor spoke.

"I got him as stable as I can, at least for now," Doc Ballen started as he wiped his forehead with his sleeve. "But he's still in pretty bad shape."

"Will he make it?" Cord decided to go ahead and ask, unwilling to wait any longer to find out.

Doc Ballen wasn't trying to hide his true thoughts as he gently shook his head. "I don't know. It's too early to say. I've never seen anyone beaten so severely and survive this long. I have to be honest with you, it doesn't look good. He has a concussion and multiple broken ribs that may or may not have collapsed a lung, not to mention the extensive damage to his face. His features are so distorted that I won't even be able to determine just how drastic that damage is until some of the swelling goes down, but I will say it's pretty bad."

"Will he make it?" Cord asked again. Cord could see that the man felt bad he couldn't give him a definitive answer.

"I honestly don't know," Doc Ballen said. "I wish I could. I'm sorry, but it's simply too early to tell." He looked over at Maddie and forced a faint smile. "Okay, miss. Now, it's your turn."

Maddie looked at Cord who threw her a reassuring smile and nod. "It's okay, Maddie. I'll be right here waiting for you." She looked at Cord and then at Doc Ballen, both of whom smiled at her. "It's okay. He'll be right here waiting for you, I promise." She followed Doc Ballen into the exam room while Cord sat back down.

Cord could not fall back asleep, not that he wanted to. He was worried about Sage and now Maddie. All of this was his fault, there was no denying it although he wished he could. He had brought all of this on his friend and her. He felt beyond horrible that he had caused them such pain because of something he had done, something that he had been asked not to get involved with, but had ignored the warnings and done so anyway. Now, two people that he cared a great deal for were both badly hurt, all because of him. One of them might even die. The thought almost made him sick.

He lingered in the waiting room for what seemed like an eternity before Doc Ballen walked back out to him. "I gave her something to help her sleep. She's resting now, but she's taken a lot of punishment. Do you know who did this to her?"

"The same man who did that to him that was looking for me," Cord admitted.

"Well, this man must want you pretty badly to inflict that kind of punishment on a woman, not to mention what he did to Sheriff Connelly."

"I've never actually met him, but from what I hear he's a pretty dangerous man."

"After seeing what he did to them I would tend to agree with you."

"Is she going to be okay?"

"Well, physically, I think so, but she took quite a beating. She has a broken nose and several deep lacerations to her face, which may or may not leave scars. Physically, she'll heal, but emotionally, that's a different story. People who experience this type of intense physical trauma could be affected by it for years, maybe even for the rest of their lives. But let's hope she comes out of this without any permanent trauma."

"Yeah."

"Oh, I almost forgot," Doc Ballen said as he reached into his pocket and pulled out a folded piece of paper and handed it to Cord. "I found this sticking out of Sheriff Connelly's shirt pocket. Thought you might know what it means."

Cord took the paper and opened it:

Spangler Ridge
Noon tomorrow

The words burned a hole in him. He glanced up as they soaked into his mind. "Doc, how long will she sleep?"

"I don't know. I'd imagine she's pretty exhausted. I'd say probably the rest of the night, maybe a little longer."

"Can she stay here till later tomorrow?"

"Yeah, it's not a problem. In fact, it would be better if she did so I could keep an eye on her. I need to look after the sheriff anyway. I have a room where she can recover. Why?"

He looked over to the doctor as he folded the note and put it in his shirt pocket. "Take care of her till I get back, will 'ya? I've got somewhere to be."

Cord Chantry woke early the following morning. He had not

slept well, but that was to be expected. All he could think about was the bounty hunter, the man who may have killed Sage and the same man who could have killed Maddie. He tried not to fixate on it, but he was unable to get the thought out of his head. He just kept picturing how brutally Sage and Maddie had been beaten, worse than almost any he had ever seen before and he had seen some pretty traumatic wounds.

After getting dressed, he fixed and ate breakfast as he thought about the man, a man whom he had never met whose job it was to bring him in to hang. A man who was hired by Judge Hess, whom he had also never met. A dangerous man. If Cord had his way Maddie and Sage would be the last ones he ever hurt. He hurried over to the doctor's office to check on Sage and Maddie.

"How are they?" He asked as Doc Ballen led him to the back room.

"Sheriff Connelly is still touch and go. He still hasn't woken up, but that's common with his type of head injury. He could be out for days. I have to be honest with you. If he happens to make it through, it'll be a miracle and even if he does it'll take him quite some time to fully heal, or as good as we can expect."

"What about Maddie?"

"See for yourself." Doc Ballen led him to a bedroom off to the side of the exam room. He opened the door slowly and allowed Cord to glance inside. Maddie was covered in the bed sleeping peacefully, a bandage wrapped around her head. The bruising to her face had gotten noticeably worse. "After I treated her wounds she passed out from the trauma and exhaustion and she hasn't woken up since. Her body had taken all it could. Right now the best thing for her is to get plenty of rest so her body has time to heal."

"Thanks, Doc. I'll come back and check on 'em later."

Cord left the doctor's office and rode the quarter horse

over to the livery stables with Jesse Morse's horse in tow and swapped out their horses for the buckskin. The animal recognized him instantly and was happy to see him, as was evident from its neighing and the nodding of its head. When he left there, he went to the sheriff's office. Sheriff Tom Wills' face said it all when he saw him walk through his door.

"Cord, what are you doing here? Are you crazy? You're a wanted man."

"I know, Tom. There's been some trouble. Sage is at Doc Ballen's office. He was almost beaten to death."

"*What?* Who did it?"

"The bounty hunter that Judge Hess hired to bring me in."

"How bad is it?"

"It's bad, Tom. Doc doesn't know if he'll make it."

"What happened?"

"I found him at his house last night."

"Oh, my gosh."

"That's not all. Maddie was beaten, too."

Tom Wills' expression fell even more than it already had. "Oh, no Cord. Is she going to be okay?"

"Doc says he thinks so. It was pretty bad."

"What kind of a sick monster would do that a woman?"

"The kind that needs to be stopped from doing it to someone else."

Tom Wills couldn't believe what he was hearing. "You're not thinking about going after this guy, are you?"

"You're damn right I am."

"Cord, I know you're upset over Maddie and Sage, but you can't do that. I've seen this guy, Cord. He's huge, probably the biggest man I've ever seen. It'd be suicide."

"I don't care," Cord responded. "He's got to be stopped. I'm just going to bring him in for the assaults."

"I don't think this man is just going to let you bring him in."

"Then I'll leave him where I find him. He might be big, but I doubt he's bulletproof."

"How will you even know how to find him?"

"He left me a note saying to meet him at Spangler Ridge at noon today."

"You could be walking into a trap, considering how this man thinks."

"Then you'll know where to recover my body."

"Cord, you can't do that."

Cord stepped closer to Tom, his anger beginning to bleed through. "He can't get away with this. If I don't stop him now he'll keep doing what he's doing and Judge Hess will keep using him and keep right on protecting him. I can't go to sleep tonight knowing I didn't at least try." Cord turned to leave and stopped himself, turning back towards Tom. "Oh, by the way, the young man in your cell is Jesse Morse."

"Yeah, I know. He was eager to tell me just as soon as I got here this morning. Where did you find him?"

"Benton Springs."

"He said you kidnapped him. He was pretty upset about it."

"I persuaded him to come to Hurley with me."

"Is that lump that he's complaining about on the back of his head your idea of persuasion?"

"Yeah, well, it got him here, didn't it?"

"He says that you kidnapped him."

"Call it what you will. The important thing is that I got him here."

"Cord, I know you want to go after this guy, but I can't let you do it. You're still a wanted man. It's my job to lock you up until we can get all of this cleared up."

"Tom, I consider you one of my only friends and I respect

what that badge stands for, I really do, but I have to do this." He turned to start for the door and heard a gun being cocked. The sound stopped him in his tracks. He didn't have to turn around to know what was happening.

"I know you're just doing your job, Tom," he spoke without turning to face him. "I respect that. If you feel like you have to shoot me then go ahead, but I'm walking out that door and I'm going after this bounty hunter." Cord paused and then started for the door. Once he had made it outside and climbed into his saddle he glanced back at the doorway where Tom was standing in the doorway, his gun holstered.

"Good luck, Cord," his friend said calmly.

Cord gave him a simple wave and a nod and then turned his horse towards Spangler Ridge. And Abel Prentiss.

CHAPTER TWENTY-TWO

As he rode into Spangler Ridge, Cord looked around for signs of the man he was there to kill.

The ridge offered an expansive view of the area which was lush with prairie Junegrass and an assortment of hardwoods. The center of the ridge offered a stunning view of the surrounding mountains, their jagged surfaces rising majestically all around and still touched with what looked like a hint of snow at their highest peaks. The sky was a crystal blue dotted with a scarcity of clouds and the air was thickening as the heat of the day continued to move in.

Cord stopped his horse just short of a simple creek which wove its way precariously through the landscape. He walked the buckskin over to the edge and allowed the animal to take in its cold, sweet freshness as he released the reins and looked around.

"I was beginning to think you weren't going to show," a booming voice called out from behind him. Cord whipped around towards the sound, his gun instantly in his hand. When he saw Abel Prentiss, he finally understood just how big he really was. He also saw that Prentiss wasn't holding a gun. "Abel Prentiss is the name."

"I wouldn't have missed this for the world," Cord said as he continued holding his gun on the man. "I had to come see the coward that likes to beat up women."

"And I had to see who has managed to upset Judge Hess so much," Prentiss replied as he repositioned a toothpick in the corner of his mouth. "I've got to say, I don't see what all the fuss is over."

"I've seen how you can beat up someone defenseless, but what about someone who hits back?"

Prentiss laughed softly. "I guess we're about to see."

Cord knew the demand was useless, but he at least had to say he tried. "You're coming in with me to answer for what you did," Cord instructed him.

"No, I don't think so, Chantry. I've got other plans."

"I don't care about your plans," Cord said fighting back the urge not to shoot the man down right there where he stood. "You need to be held accountable."

"And you think you're the one to do that?" Prentiss said mockingly, following by a simple laugh. "Better men than you have tried and failed. What makes you think you'll do any better?"

"Maybe they didn't want to kill you bad enough."

"And you do?"

"Yeah, I do," Cord said as he continued to glare at the man.

Prentiss took a couple of steps towards him and stopped. "Then do it."

Cord continued to stare at Prentiss, still holding his gun on him as he fought the urge not to squeeze his trigger finger. His resistance was strong, but he wasn't sure if it was strong enough. He hesitated, wanting so much to go through with it, but in the end he just couldn't bring himself to be a killer, even to the likes of Prentiss. Cord watched a smile form on Prentiss' face.

"I knew you couldn't do it." Prentiss scoffed. "How's the sheriff?" he asked, his question smothered with sarcasm.

"He might die because of you."

"And his wife?"

Cord felt his hand tensing up as he fought the urge to shoot. His anger was boiling inside him. "That wasn't his wife. She's with me."

Prentiss let out a boisterous laugh. "So she's with you?" Prentiss said as he continued laughing, making Cord more and more angry. "I can't believe that. A pretty little thing like that with a loser like you? It's unheard of."

"Why'd you have to do it, Prentiss? Why'd you have to try to kill them?"

"Oh, I wasn't trying to kill them," Prentiss corrected him. "If I had, they'd be dead now. No, I was only trying to get to you. I was tired of chasing you all over the territory so I decided to do something to ensure that you came to me."

"You still didn't have to beat up Maddie."

"Oh, right *that's* her name. Well, she didn't tell me what her name was, but now that you mention it I do remember the sheriff saying it right before I beat his brains in."

"I should kill you right now," Cord said coldly.

"Then do it," Prentiss ridiculed him for the second time.

Cord hesitated, his jaw clinching from the pressure.

Prentiss scoffed loudly. "I knew you didn't have it in you, Chantry," Prentiss taunted him. "You're weak, and that's what's going to get you killed."

"I'm not weak, but unlike you I don't take advantage of others."

"It's called 'opportunity'," Prentiss pointed out, "and it's the reason why you'll fail today because you didn't take advantage of it when you had the chance. Of course, it's hard to prove that when you're hiding behind that gun of yours."

Cord holstered his gun and continued staring at Prentiss. "I'm not here to fail," he said as he slowly unbuckled his gun belt and dropped it onto the ground beside him. The gesture made Prentiss' smile even larger. Cord watched as the man unbuckled his own gun belt and dropped it.

"I don't need a gun," Prentiss declared as he tossed away his toothpick. "I'll kill you the old fashioned way."

Cord started cautiously walking towards Prentiss, eying him carefully. The man was big, that was for certain. He had never fought a man this size. He had two inches on Cord and a good thirty pounds. His shoulders were wide and thick, his hands the size of small plates. Cord sized him up as they neared one another and began to be concerned. There was no way he could match Prentiss' strength. If he tried to he would surely fail. The man was no doubt strong, just how strong he was afraid to find out which meant he had to stay away from his grip. If the man ever got his hands on him Cord feared he wouldn't be able to break free. He had seen what Prentiss could do to a man and that was when he had allowed Sage to live. How much harder would he be on someone that he was hellbent on killing?

As the men came within range of one another, Cord waited for Prentiss to make the first move. He didn't have to wait long.

Prentiss threw a right which Cord saw coming and was partially able to move out of the way. The blow didn't make good contact, but it still managed to hit enough of Cord to partially stun him. Cord immediately swung wide catching Prentiss on the jaw, which Prentiss quickly shook off and reached for the front of Cord's shirt. There was still enough distance between them for Cord to duck out of the way leaving Prentiss off-balance and grabbing at thin air. As Cord weaved off to the side he delivered a sharp punch to his ribs, but before he could follow it with another punch a massive right hand came crashing down onto the side of Cord's skull. This one made contact and temporarily stunned Cord like he'd been struck with a sledgehammer, but to his surprise Prentiss did not follow it up with another punch. Instead he stood his ground firmly. He was toying with Cord.

"I'm gonna take my time with you," Prentiss bragged. As he smiled, he somewhat relaxed his posture and Cord took the opportunity and stepped in with a sharp jab to the chin and then a right and a left. Prentiss was not amused at being caught off guard as his smile quickly faded. He slowly reached up and touched his lip, pulling his hand back to see blood on his fingers from his split lip. He glanced up at Cord, unamused. "It's been a long time since I've bled."

Cord continuing eying the man with cool contempt. "Get used to it."

Prentiss lunged forward swinging. The first punch took Cord's head off to the side and he continued with another right in the same spot and then one to his gut. The force of the punch was able to knock the wind out of Cord. He tried to step back long enough to regain his breathing, but Prentiss was already on him again. He reached over and grabbed the front of Cord's shirt and pulled him closer and began punching again and again with his right, each blow easily finding its mark and each one staggering Cord's alertness. With no time to recover between blows, his thinking was beginning to get distorted with each passing second.

He had failed to keep away from his grasp. Cord knew he was in trouble.

Prentiss had pulled his fist back to deliver another powerful punch when Cord jabbed his right into Prentiss' throat as hard as he could. The punch caught Prentiss by surprise and forced him to loosen his grip on Cord's shirt as he clutched the front of his neck as he wheezed in sharply, coughing and gagging. As soon as he felt the man's hand loosen Cord pulled away just far enough to swing a right to Prentiss' face. The hit was a solid one and along with the blow to his throat jarred him just long enough for Cord to plant his feet firmly and go in swinging.

Cord caught Prentiss on the side of his face and then delivered a solid right and another equally-damaging left, hoping to continue his assault, but by now Prentiss had already begun to recover from the surprise blow to his throat and came in angry. *He had underestimated Cord the first time,* he thought. *He would make sure not to make that mistake again.*

Prentiss barreled forward fending off Cord's punches and landing one of his own to stun him just long enough to grab him in a bear hug. He clamped his hands together tightly around his waist and began squeezing. Cord groaned in anguish as Prentiss tightened his grip more, forcing the air out of Cord and preventing him from breathing properly, forcing him to resort to taking in short, shallow breaths. Cord began to panic. He desperately tried to free himself, but Prentiss was simply too strong to overcome. Cord's worst fears were suddenly coming true. His back began to scream out in agony as he felt his ribs being crushed from the back. He strained with everything he had pushing against Prentiss' chest with all his might, but Prentiss' grip was simply too powerful to be broken.

The physical exhaustion from the fighting combined with not being able to take in deep enough breaths was quickly taking its toll on Cord. He began to feel light-headed as his brain was slowly being deprived of much-needed oxygen as he felt Prentiss' grip becoming even tighter. His resistance was becoming weaker, a sign that Prentiss recognized causing him to squeeze even harder, his teeth gritting from the pressure. Cord knew he had only seconds before he passed out.

With one final effort he opened his arms as wide as they would go and slapped his hands as hard as he could onto Prentiss' ears, bursting both eardrums. The intense pain caused Prentiss to release his grip on Cord as he took a step back and screamed, clamping his hands over his ears which were already beginning to drip with blood. He leaned his head back, the pain excruciating, the incessant ringing in his head causing him to feel as if it would split his skull. Cord had taken the opportunity to regain his breath as best he could. He saw his chance.

With his last remaining strength, Cord lunged at Prentiss, driving his head into his gut with all his force. Prentiss was so consumed with trying to dull the agonizing pain in his head that he was not expecting the move. The resounding rush of air leaving Prentiss' lungs was just the clue Cord had been waiting for. He had found Prentiss' weakness. He might not be able to overpower Prentiss' immense strength, but he now knew that his only chance of surviving this was to work on his midsection.

Cord stepped in and laid a series of punches directly into Prentiss' ribs, first on one side and then the other. Prentiss tried to release his hands from off of his ears long enough to fight back, but he was still in too much pain to concentrate as much as was needed. He managed to get off a punch, though considerably weaker than his others, but Cord deflected most of it away, causing it to lose most of its effectiveness.

The turn of events encouraged Cord even more as he continued pounding away at Prentiss' midsection again and again with everything he had, slowly wearing the man down, each blow almost doubling Prentiss over in pain. Cord was exhausted, but he dared not stop now. *This would be the only chance he had*, he told himself. He continued working on Prentiss landing one solid blow after another. Prentiss tried as best as he could to protect his midsection, but Cord was relentless in his attack and was not giving him the chance to fight back. The barrage of punches to his midsection was distorting Prentiss' breathing and slowly draining his strength, lowering his defenses. He periodically managed to make contact with a weakened punch, but Cord was able to shake them off and continue his attack. For the first time ever, Prentiss could see that he was in trouble.

Cord fired away with everything he had until the big man could no longer stand the constant abuse and fell to one knee. Though still swinging errant punches he continued to groan in agony as Cord abandoned his gut and began relentlessly tearing away at his face without mercy, his punches slowly chipping away at Prentiss' resistance. He opened Prentiss' left eye releasing a gush of blood down his face and continued working on his jaw. Finally, the assault was too much for him and Prentiss' other leg gave way and he slumped to the ground onto his knees facing Cord, his head weaving slightly from side to side, his eyes glassed over and empty. Cord pulled back and swung a hard right with everything he had hitting Prentiss squarely on the jaw and knocking him over like a felled tree.

He stood over the big man, his arms having fallen by his sides and completely spent. He was almost too exhausted to breathe as he fought to take in air in deep, rapid gulps. His back was in excruciating pain, still reeling from Prentiss' bear hug and his shirt soaked with sweat all the way down to his waist. He struggled to stay on his feet, his balance and strength all but used up, his resolve pushed to its limit.

He stumbled over to his gun belt, almost falling more than once from the weakness in his legs while taking his time to reach down to recover it. He had buckled his gun belt and was slowly reaching down for his hat when he heard Prentiss yell behind him. He had spun around just in time to see Prentiss running at him with his knife in his hand, a look of unimaginable rage spread over his face when he drew. His hand was shaking from exhaustion as he fanned out four shots in rapid succession, all of them hitting their mark in the center of Prentiss' body. The man's face glossed over and his eyes opened wide. He clutched his chest and ceased taking steps as he fell to his knees and then flat onto the ground. Cord dropped to the ground, a thin trail of smoke rising from his gun as a wave of relief cascaded over him.

CHAPTER TWENTY-THREE

The outer door to Judge Hess' chambers flew open as three men walked in single file. Judge Hess' clerk, Leonard Baker, was caught by surprise and jumped up from his chair with an agitated look. "What are you doing? You can't just barge in there like this!" he said loudly. The first two men passed by him without giving him a second glance while the third one of the group, Tom Wills, said nothing and hit Leonard with a hard right that knocked the man backwards bouncing him off of his chair and onto the floor. The first two men opened the door to Judge Hess' chambers and walked on in without announcing their presence.

"What is the meaning of this!" Judge Hess shouted as he quickly stood. "Leonard! Leonard! Get in here and remove these men, now!"

"I don't think Leonard is going to be able to help you anytime soon, judge," Tom Wills informed him as he joined the other men who had stopped in front of the judge's desk.

"What are you doing barging into my office like this?!" Judge Hess shouted at the men.

Cord stepped over to the side of his desk and forcibly

pushed the judge back down into his chair. "Sit down and shut up," he instructed him.

"You can't talk to me like that!" he spouted as he looked over at the first man. "And who the hell are you?!"

"Names Cord Chantry," Cord advised him calmly.

"*Cord Chantry?!*" Judge Hess yelled as he abruptly stood. "Why, you're a killer! I'll have you..."

Cord shoved him back into his chair again, this time with more force. He stared at the man with his light grey eyes. "Get up again and you'll be picking your teeth up off of the floor."

Judge Hess shuffled in his chair from anger. "Who do you think you are, barging in here and threatening me?!"

"I'll tell you who *I* am, Judge Hess," said the second man. "I'm Clayton Foster, federal marshal for the Wyoming territory."

"*Federal marshal?* What on earth are *you* doing here? I didn't send for you."

"No, *I* did," Tom Wills chimed in. "I wired him back when all of this started."

"You had no right to do that," Judge Hess scolded Tom Wills. "I run the show around here!"

"Not anymore," Marshal Foster spoke. "You're being relieved of your duties effective immediately pending a full investigation.'

Judge Hess' face turned red from rage. "What kind of investigation?!"

"Hiring a bounty hunter to hunt down Mr. Chantry here, for one, under the guise that he would be hanged without due process."

"I never said anything about that," Judge Hess denied profusely.

"Yeah, you did. Sheriff Connelly is a witness to it. You told him right here in this office."

Judge Hess shook his head adamantly. "I don't know anything about a bounty hunter."

"Wrong again, judge," Tom Wills responded as he retrieved a piece of paper from his pocket and held it up for the judge to see. "Remember this? It's the note you wrote for Abel Prentiss to give to me to pump me for information on where he could find Cord."

"I wrote no such note!" Hess insisted.

"That's funny because this is your signature on it right here," Tom said as he turned the note to face Judge Hess. Hess' temper began to diminish as he realized he was done for.

"Well, if you don't believe me then bring this Abel Prentiss in here and ask him yourself!"

"I'm afraid that's not going to happen, either," Cord spoke. "Prentiss is still out at Spangler Ridge, at least whats left of him now that the wolves and mountain lions have been feeding off of him."

Judge Hess slumped back in his chair, a look of utter defeat overwhelming him. He sat speechless.

"Let's go, Hess," Marshal Foster said as he walked around the desk and grabbed Hess by the arm and forcibly lifted him out of the chair. As he escorted the disgraced judge past Cord, Hess glared at the man without saying a word.

Two weeks later...

It was another steamy morning in Hurley as the door to the sheriff's office opened and Cord Chantry and Madeline Stafford walked in to find Sage Connelly sitting behind the desk.

"Morning, Sage," Cord greeted him.

"Good morning, Sage," Maddie added with a smile as they stopped in front of his desk.

"Morning, Maddie. Cord," Sage responded with a smile, acknowledging each one separately. "What brings ya'll out this fine morning?"

"Oh, I just came into town to pick up some supplies and Maddie asked if she could ride along," Cord resounded with his own smile. "How are you feeling?"

"I've about mended, I guess," Sage commented. "Y'know, I got to thinking the other day. Every time you come around, I get hurt. It's beginning to seem like being your friend is bad for my health."

The three laughed at the comment. "Well, it hasn't been a picnic for me, either," Cord admitted. "It's a good thing I'm tough."

"Yeah," Sage answered, "How are you doing, Maddie?"

Her expression somewhat softened from the question, but she still maintained a faint smile. "I'm okay. I suppose it just takes a little bit of time to get over these things," she said as she glanced over to Cord who responded with a smile.

"Glad to hear it," Sage responded. "Say, Cord, have you heard from Jesse Morse lately?"

"Not since he testified. Once he gave his testimony to the federal marshal he high-tailed it out of town and that was the last I saw of him."

Sage chuckled. "Yeah, I don't think you made a friend there, that's for sure."

Cord glanced around the office. "Hey, where's Tom?"

"He's over at the restaurant getting him some lunch."

"Lunch?" Cord said curiously. "It's mid-morning."

"There's a girl that works over there that he's sweet on. Names Laura."

"Does she know?" Maddie asked jokingly.

Sage chuckled. "Yeah, and she's crazy about him, too."

"Sounds like love is in the air," Maddie implied.

"Well, we gotta go," Cord announced. "I promised the man over at the freight office that I'd pick my supplies up before noon."

"Thanks for dropping by, you two," Sage said as he stood and shook hands with Cord.

"See ya' later, Sage."

"Maddie," Sage said with a nod.

"Sheriff," she responded, smiling.

Sage Connelly smiled and watched Cord and Maddie leave the office and sat back down into his chair. Before he could get back to his paperwork, Tom Wills walked in. "Hey, sheriff," he said as he turned and pointed behind him, "I just saw Cord and Maddie."

"Yeah, they were just in here. They stopped by to see how I was doing."

"Did they notice that you were sheriff again?"

"Yeah. They already knew, but I still think you should have kept this, Tom."

Tom Wills shook his head as he sat. "No, it belongs with you. I'm not cut out to be a sheriff, just yet. I'm happy being a deputy, at least for the time being."

"Well," Sage spoke,"I told Cord if I keep hanging around with him you'll get your chance soon enough," he said as the two men laughed.

The wagon carrying Cord and Maddie was headed down the streets of Hurley when he pulled it over and stopped in front of the restaurant.

"What are we stopping for?" Maddie asked, confused. "It's too early for lunch."

"I know," Cord said with a mischievous smile. "Just wait here. I'll be right back."

Maddie watched as Cord disappeared inside the restaurant only to emerge a few minutes later carrying a basket. He placed the basket in the back of the wagon and climbed back into the seat. As he grabbed the reins and urged the horse into motion Maddie could no longer stifle her curiosity. "What's in the basket? What's going on, Cord?"

Cord flashed his mischievous grin. "I'm taking you on a picnic."

She looked at him curiously. "A picnic? What's the occasion?"

Cord's grin broadened. "I need to talk to you about something."